I don't think I'm ev... ...off the asphalt.

I come to when a boot smashes into my stomach and a lightning-gash of pain tears through my gut. I struggle out of the darkness into consciousness, like a drowning man gasping for air. I gasp for the light in my eyes and somehow he's still there and like a nightmare it's happening again and again and now I'm on my back and he's an Indian in war paint or he's a tiger now and he's growling and my whole body's on fire and I hear him snarl something about staying away from Pintler—then he says it clearly, stay away or die—and he smashes his boot into me again and it's like a steel hammer hitting a glass mirror and my mind goes skittering away in a thousand jagged pieces.

— ★ —

Previously published Worldwide Mystery title by
JOHN PAXSON

BONES

A GOLDEN TRAIL OF
MURDER

JOHN PAXSON

WORLDWIDE.

TORONTO • NEW YORK • LONDON
AMSTERDAM • PARIS • SYDNEY • HAMBURG
STOCKHOLM • ATHENS • TOKYO • MILAN
MADRID • WARSAW • BUDAPEST • AUCKLAND

A GOLDEN TRAIL OF MURDER

A Worldwide Mystery/May 2003

First published by Thomas Bouregy & Company, Inc.

ISBN 0-373-26455-0

Printed in U.S.A.

For world-class geologists Dr. Steven Bussey and
Dr. Katherine Connors—
and the elusive orbicular trout.

ONE

THE OLD MAN came awake slowly from a restless night. In the yellow half-light of the room, the familiar ticking of the alarm clock seemed muffled by the fury of the wind screaming outside. He moved stiffly across the cold floor and pushed apart the curtains, rubbing a callused palm at the spiders of ice that had crept up the frosted pane. Beyond, the morning was lost in a chaos of blowing greys and whites. The log barn appeared as an uncertain dark smudge through the consuming blizzard and the winter-bare trunks of the cottonwood trees quivered and bent like thin grey bones with each new blast of snow and ice.

The old man thought about the drifts that would be forming out along the coulees, drifts that could founder a horse, could destroy a herd—or kill a man. He gave off a quiet involuntary shudder under his long underwear as he thought about the times he'd ridden into the teeth of such weather to try to save what he could of cattle that had bunched up against a fence line for cover only to be swallowed in the suffocating white confusion. He'd always carried an empty burlap sack in his saddle bags. The rough cloth was good for rubbing life back into new-born calves—or lost hunters—freezing to death in the impersonal rage of a Montana blizzard. Sometimes it wasn't enough. The old man absently blew into his hands, as though to warm them.

The telephone ringing in the kitchen brought him back.

His curt "hello" echoed around the empty room and he listened for a minute. "Damned bad weather to be out in," he said. More listening. "When'd he go?" His voice had in it a deep fatigue and a small edge of concern. "He's smart enough not to do that." He was interrupted and held the phone to his ear for a time without speaking. "How far up?" More listening. "He's not that stupid. But I'll see if the truck starts, take a look."

The old man brewed a pot of coffee, gathered a few things he'd need, and bundled himself heavily against the blizzard. Outside, the cold air burned like a sulphur match as it hit his lungs and the wind attacked his face like blasts of frozen buckshot. He shrugged his head deep into his coat and pulled his wool cap down so it almost covered his eyes. Squinting against the wind, he made his way slowly to the barn and pried open its big doors, silently cursing the errand that would take him out on such a day.

To his mild surprise, the old truck started on the first try. He revved the engine and set the heater on high, his fingers stiff and painful inside wool and leather mittens, the plastic seat cover as hard as plywood under him. His breath hung like heavy morning fog in the frigid cab.

Almost reluctantly, he shifted the truck into sub-low and nosed it steadily out into the storm. The wind hammered at the cab and thick snow matted the windshield. The tires bit into the drifts with a squealing crunch and the old man fed on more gas and the truck plowed like a small boat through the storm. At the end of the lane, it bucked hard as it plunged through a low wall of plowed snow but then he was on the main road and the snow was packed hard and he was moving.

Or the speedometer said he was moving. With the wind to his back now, the snow was travelling at roughly his speed and he had the sensation that the truck was almost standing still, or being pushed slowly along in the center of an impatient white cloud. He scraped with his mittened hands at the frost on the windshield.

He had been driving maybe ten minutes when a pair of blinking amber lights materialized ahead in the grey gloom. He slowed the truck and the snow whipped past. A stalled car appeared from the white swirl and the old man brought the truck to a delicate stop, taking care to avoid a skid that would put him into the ravine that lay unseen to the side of the road. His errand would have to wait.

The figure of a man detached itself from the shape of the car and approached through the storm. Flying snow and bitter cold rolled in as the old man cracked open the window.

"Howdy," shouted the muffled figure over the roar of the wind. He was wrapped in a heavy sheepskin coat and his eyes peered out from two slits in a stocking cap that covered his head and face. The frosted hole around his mouth showed a glimpse of skin oddly discolored, as though smudged with charcoal or paint.

"What's the problem?" the old man yelled through the window.

"Stalled on me."

The old man climbed down stiffly from the truck, squinting his eyes against the flying snow.

The bundled figure had popped the hood and was examining the engine. The old man came up beside him and bent over to peer inside. "Maybe you flooded it?" he shouted over the wind.

The blow took him just above the temple—a brief stunning impact across the side of his forehead that froze his senses. There was no time for pain: a sharp crushing blow, a lightning-fast moment of confusion, bewilderment, and the old man crumpled onto the packed snow of the roadway.

The bundled figure moved quickly. Lifting the unconscious body by the arms, he dragged it back to the truck and managed to hoist and shove it into the cab. Bracing the door open against the wind, the figure reached across the old man and shifted the truck into gear. He gave the gas pedal a push and cramped the steering wheel hard right and jumped free as the truck began to roll forward toward the ravine.

The truck bucked through the low snow bank at the road's edge and pitched over, gaining speed as it rolled into the deep gully. Halfway down, its nose spun upward and the truck flipped over, sliding the last few yards in a cloud of snow and ice before settling on its side into the bottom of the ravine. The engine coughed and died. In minutes, the drifts had begun to form like a soft white sheet across a cold metal coffin. The bundled man and his stalled car were miles away when the last trace of the old rancher and his icy tomb were swallowed by the swirling winter snow.

TWO

I WAS WELL INTO a morning's work and had actually managed to break a sweat in the cool spring air when Nate Bowen's green Jeep rattled across the metal cattle guard. I was framing out an addition on my cabin to make space for a new bedroom with a wide window that would look out across the barn and pasture to the high mountains that ring the narrow meadow I call home. I didn't need the room much but over the years had come to obsess on the idea of it, telling friends about it so many times that I'd finally gotten to the point where I had to put up or shut up. I was thinking about that tendency of painting myself into corners as Bowen's tires banged across the cattle guard like a machine gun on the quiet mountain air. I slipped the hammer into the leather work apron and headed down the ladder.

"How're those walls, partner?" Bowen boomed in a deep, friendly voice. "That new addition still sagging south on you?" A small smile cracked his weathered face as he moved a big hand through his hair. I'd often wondered if nature hadn't made a mistake with Nate Bowen, if she hadn't somehow managed to mix in a few black bear genes when she was brewing him up. He and I were about the same height, a little over six feet, but where I was lean, he was thick—not fat thick, but thick like a bear. And where I had blond hair headed toward grey, his was a stubborn coarse black, almost like fur. That and a rolling amble of a walk and quick dark eyes that sat a little too close together gave pause to people who didn't know he was one of the most gentle men around. Those eyes seemed hooded and a little tired this morning. "Anything to drink in this frontier outpost of yours?"

"A visit from Bowen, huh?" I said. "Buy you a tea?" I got a nod and low mutter.

The two of us settled at the table I'd rigged up under the elderly pine that fronts the cabin. Beyond, the three horses who share the place with me were picking at the pale carpet of new meadow grass coming green out the winter snows. Back in the trees, a few remnant snow drifts were dissolving slowly into the brown pine needles and red earth. The air had a new-season scent of fresh pine and wet loam.

"Strange to have cold drinks this early in the year," said Bowen, toasting his ice tea in my direction. "Montana's not supposed to be this warm in April. Figure there's maybe something to all that hot air about global warming."

I shrugged. "Say it's the warmest spring in fifteen or twenty years. Snow's coming down fast up high. Rivers are way up."

Bowen nodded absently and looked past me toward the distant tree line where the peaks of the Rockies still brooded grey under a stained white blanket of winter snow. "Got a bad phone call last night." The lines of his face seemed pinched.

"Trouble?"

"Hard to say at this point." Bowen took a long pull

on the tea and wiped his mouth with the sleeve of his blue cotton shirt. "Got a call from Mike."

"Mike...?"

"Woolsey," said Bowen.

It took me a minute to pull the name up. "The kid who fell in?"

"Same one."

Ten years before, a quiet trout stream and a wet boy shivering. "He ever learn to fish?" I asked.

Bowen nodded. "Not half bad."

Mike Woolsey was some sort of distant cousin to Bowen. He'd been just a scruff of a kid—probably eight or nine—when Bowen had decided he needed fishing lessons and roped me on the project. One thing led to another, Bowen disappeared downstream, and the next thing I knew the kid's fly line was wrapped like a yarn ball in a willow tree and the boy had managed to fall in the river. I'd spent a whole afternoon untangling things and drying him out—and thinking malicious thoughts about my friend Nate Bowen.

"He still asks about you," Bowen said.

"Nice kid."

"Not much of a kid anymore," said Bowen. "Almost twenty."

"Hard to believe."

"Got pretty good with a fly rod. Still credits it to you. Go figure."

"Things ever get any better with his father?"

Bowen shook his head. "Still bad blood there."

I knew, vaguely, that Bowen had helped the boy along over the years but didn't give a tinker's damn for the rest of the kid's family. Bowen had never said why and I'd never asked. The family lived down toward the border near Idaho, outside a town called Pintler.

"Anyway, Mike phoned last night," said Bowen. "Pretty big headline. They found his granddad frozen in a snow drift."

I let out a soft whistle, more in sympathy than surprise. People can manage to die a lot of ways and freezing to death in a Montana winter's not particularly original. "Tough way to go."

Bowen nodded and studied his tea.

"How'd he manage to get in a drift?"

Bowen seemed to roll it over in his mind. "That's an odd one. Mike says his grandfather turned up missing late January and everybody suspected the worst. Truck gone. No sign of him. Big storm at the time. Heavy drifts. They searched his ranch and all around. Had the county search and rescue out. Dogs, helicopter. Not a trace of him. Tough country up there. And real tough to search in winter."

"Strange."

"Yeah, strange. I guess a lot of things can disappear into a Montana blizzard. Anyway, he did. The drifts started coming down a couple of weeks ago and they found the truck not too far from the ranch on its side at the bottom of a pretty good gully. Him inside it. Stiff as a plank."

"Cold way to die."

Bowen nodded. "Real cold way to die. Had a bump on his head. Looks like the truck slid off the road, he got knocked out and froze to death before he came to. That's the way the locals see it."

The two of us sat in silence for a while, Bowen looking out at the mountains in a distracted sort of way, I trying to imagine what it'd be like to freeze to death like that. It made me cold on a warm spring day.

"Mike thinks somebody killed him," said Bowen. He glanced up with a flat-eyed look that gave away little.

"Reasons?"

"Good question, partner. But Mike says old Carson Woolsey was a very careful man...the sort of man who wouldn't have driven himself off a road in a blizzard. And from what I know of him I tend to agree. He was a crusty old fart."

"Cops?"

"Did sort of a half-baked investigation." Bowen paused, as though thinking over what he'd just said. "Well, I suppose that's not fair. They investigated it. Find an old guy off the road in a blizzard, draw your own conclusions. The coroner agrees with the cops. Nothing suspicious about it, according to them. Trouble's the boy, Mike. Says his grandfather didn't make it to nearly eighty by being a careless man. He tried getting them to re-open the case. They won't do it."

"Who does he think did it?"

"Told me he doesn't know." Bowen paused. "The kid can't figure it."

"And the kid wants your help?" I knew Bowen's help meant my help too: in another life before the mountains pulled me back, I'd made a living uncovering other people's crimes, 25 years of it. I still did it, but only once in a while when my small ranch and the big mountains got to be too much...or too little.

"'Bout the size of it," said Bowen with a verbal shrug. "I think it's a bit off, myself. Sounds to me like the old boy had one very mortal accident. I told Mike that. But he's a persistent little snot." Bowen offered the comment with a squinted eye and a thin smile. "Guess it runs in the family. He harangued me almost to death on the phone. Told him I run a sporting-goods store—I sell rifles, fishing rods, things like that. I don't investigate murders. But he kept at me and I finally said I'd see what I could do. Told him I knew this guy Ben Tripp. Not much of a fishing guide, but a pretty good private eye." Bowen's dark eyes did a quick two-step across the new bedroom taking shape above us. "You doin' anything important right now?"

I followed his glance to the raw timbers jutting out of the roof. Bowen and I had seen a lot together and over the years he'd asked little of me beyond friendship. That he was asking now meant it had to be important. I brought my gaze back down to the big man across the table from me. "Let's go find your cousin."

THREE

IT WAS APPARENT as Bowen and I drove into the town the next morning that Pintler was doing pretty well these days: The new Montana chic had obviously been good for its three thousand souls. The shabby clapboard sidings I'd remembered from earlier years had been replaced by trendy log walls on new shops the length of the three-block main drag. A couple of tourist stands with Indian souvenirs poked out amid quickstop mini-marts and real estate offices. Crow war bonnets and Navajo blankets offered a colonial stupidity in the land of the Blackfoot and Nez Perce. A rock shop proclaimed real gold in fake gold paint.

I've always had trouble sorting out the area around Pintler. As the last dot on the map before Highway 93 climbs into the Rockies and disappears into the Salmon River country of Idaho, the town had always been a kind of isolated frontier outpost. Spectacularly jagged mountains and heavy forests pitch down to a narrow river valley in cascading confusions of granite cliffs, thick forests, and sudden mountain streams. A wild, reckless beauty that's nice to look at, dangerous to touch. People who live there seem a lot like that themselves—friendly enough to the outsiders passing through but wrapped in the fabric of a private world that few outsiders could enter. Difficult, cautious lives lived behind hard rock and heavy timber.

Bowen guided us to a place called the Sunshine Bar. Muddy pickup trucks with oversized tires were parked outside and two loaded logging trucks idled in a narrow slush-covered alley next door. Inside, loud voices and cigarette smoke mingled with the smell of frying hamburgers and stale beer. A room of plaid wool shirts glanced briefly our way as we waded to a table near the rear where a young man with red hair sat sipping a Coke.

Mike Woolsey was a grown-up version of the boy I remembered—thin, almost scrawny, a long face under surprised blue eyes, ears a touch too large and pale skin that probably kept him out of the sun. His mouth, though, had a set to it I didn't remember. It made me think there might be some fight under the sallow surface.

"You remember Ben Tripp?" said Bowen.

A thin smile grew across the boy's slim face. "Sure do," he said. "Hello Mr. Tripp." The boy's handshake was unexpectedly strong.

"Howdy, Mike, and you know my name's Ben. How's fishin'?"

The boy grinned at the question.

"Seems hard to figure it's been ten years," I said.

"Your granddad was a good man," said Bowen. "You doing okay?"

The boy turned his face away to hide the abrupt softening in his eyes and I felt embarrassed for him. Bowen took his thin shoulder in one big hand. "Steady there, partner. Tough times but we'll get you through 'em." Bowen caught my eye and nodded his head toward the bar.

I made my way across the packed room and ordered a couple of beers. The big-bellied bartender seemed friendly. "Passin' through?"

"Meetin' a friend," I offered vaguely.

The bartender glanced toward the table where Nate and Mike were talking quietly. "Tough for the kid," the man said and ran his hands down the front of his clean white apron. "Worthless family but Mike turned out all right. They say him and the old man were pretty close."

"Heard about it, huh?"

"Whole valley's heard about it," offered the bartender as he wiped at an imaginary spot on the glistening wood counter. "Whole valley's got ideas about it, too."

"And the valley says?"

"Just strange, is all," said the bartender. "Who'd figure Carson getting his candle snuffed in a drift."

"Accident?"

The bartender lowered his gaze and ran a hand through his thin black hair. "That's a tough one to call. Something's going on. Been some strangers through here we haven't seen before." He wiped at the spot again. "S'pect if I was an interested party, I'd figure out what others are up to in these parts. Guys in army fatigues who like guns." He glanced up with a hard look that he obviously hoped would seem tough and knowing, but it came across instead as shifty and nervous.

"What are you saying?"

The bartender dropped his eyes quickly and gave the imaginary spot another pass with his rag. "Just been some outsiders through more than once is all. Real strange guys. But none of my business." The man moved off down the bar. I made my way back across the room and sat down at the table.

"Mike's basically filled me in on what he knows," said Bowen, and the boy beside him nodded. "Pretty much what we talked about. Out in a bad blizzard—no one knows why—and down into a big ravine. Everybody says car accident, except Mike here."

With some gentle prodding from Bowen, Mike began to talk about the ranch, the family, his grandfather.

A Woolsey had opened the land just after the Civil War. Carson Woolsey himself had run it for 60-plus years, outliving his wife and raising one son, Edward—Mike's father. Edward lived in town with his second wife, sold insurance, and visited the old man on the occasional Sunday, though he and Carson were not close. Mostly it was the boy Mike who was the link between the generations.

"It's been like that since I can remember," said Mike. "Summers on the ranch, weekends. I stayed in town with my folks to go to school during the winter. But pretty much every spare minute I could find I'd manage to get out there." Bowen and I encouraged him with nods.

"It seemed like such a unbelievable place to me," said Mike. "The cattle, the horses. Grandpa had me up in a saddle from about the time I could walk." A tentative smile slid across his face. "He always said that for a gawky kid with too many freckles, I made a pretty good ranch hand."

"You work here in town now?"

"At the grocery store," said Mike. "I did the first semester at the university in Bozeman, but then when this happened, well, I dropped out for a while. Got an apartment—actually it's just a room at the motel but it's enough.''

"Is your mother around?"

The boy's eyes took on a hooded look and his words seemed careful. ''She works at the cafe at the north end of town.''

"You don't stay with her?"

"We're not close."

"What about your dad?"

"What about him?"

"You don't stay with him?"

The boy let off with a snort. ''Not likely. His second wife doesn't think much of me.''

"Seems kinda tough," I said, my tone gentle. ''You're not very close to either your mom or your dad?''

The boy shrugged his shoulders. ''Just worked out that way. Grandpa's always been there.'' The comment dropped the table into silence.

"Nathan tells me this all happened late January?'' I said after a while—more to break the awkward silence than to actually get information.

"The third week of January," said Mike. ''I was getting ready to go back to school from winter break. My dad called and said Grandpa had disappeared.''

"Who found the truck?"

"A road crew plowing snow saw a tire sticking up.''

"That was when?"

"A couple of weeks ago," said Mike. ''We buried him last week.''

"Any idea what he was doing out there?" I asked.

"None," said the boy, ''and that's the problem. The weather was real bad—way too bad for anybody to go out in it if they didn't have to. There just wasn't a reason for him to be out there.''

I spent a bit of time explaining myself—that beyond being a fishing instructor for small boys once in a while, I occasionally looked into things for people but didn't carry an investigator's license, or a gun. I told him this case was on the house, a favor for old times, and he seemed relieved.

"Your granddad have any enemies?" I asked. "I mean the sort who'd do something like that?"

Mike took a while answering and when he finally did it came out slowly, thoughtfully. "There was nothing like that. He got along with everybody—and it's not like there are a lot of people out there. It's remote. And everybody has to help each other. I mean they're ranchers. They may not like each other a lot but when times get bad they all stick together. So, no, nothing like that.''

"You know the neighbors?"

"Most of them," said the boy. "Like I said, it's pretty remote. Closest is a fellow named Summey, Joe Summey. He's been up there forever. The others are newer and I don't think Grandpa knows them"—the boy hesitated—"knew them all that well.''

I made a mental note to find the neighbor Summey. Across the room the bartender was still busy pulling beers from the tap. "Your granddad ever involved in the militia," I asked, "anything like that?"

Mike offered a sharp, joyless laugh. "The militia? He wouldn't give those guys the time of day. He said they were a bunch of jackass kids who liked to play war.''

I leaned back in my seat. Kids who liked to play war were managing to make a few headlines, none of them good—and I considered dangerous anybody with paranoia and a gun. "They're around, though?" I asked. Bowen gave me a questioning look from across the table.

"Yeah, they've been around," said Mike. "You hear 'em shooting sometimes from the ranch. I think they train somewhere back in the mountains. But Granddad never took them very seriously."

"You ever see any of them? What I mean is, your grandfather ever have anything to do with them, face-to-face, that sort of thing?"

Mike shook his head. "Maybe we'd hear them. Or maybe it was hunters. We never paid much attention."

I studied my nearly empty beer, trying to sort through the information, the hints, the possibilities. No matter how I looked at it, the whole thing seemed thin. "You still think it wasn't an accident?"

Mike looked up from his Coke and took his time answering. When they finally came out, the words were deliberate. "I don't think the militia had anything to do with it, if that's what you mean. But yeah, it wasn't an accident. Granddad wouldn't die that stupidly." His voice had about it a tone of certainty and finality.

FOUR

BACK OUTSIDE, Bowen and I were headed for the sheriff's office a couple of blocks away when we heard
the scream of an ambulance from the main highway.
We both stopped and drew back as it flew down the
street past us and pulled up in a shower of slush and
flying mud in front of a low brick building. There was
a flurry of activity as the rear doors were thrown open
and a couple of people struggled to pull out a stretcher.
They were obviously having troubles and I ran down
the street.

An attendant was fumbling to lock the legs under
the gurney which kept pitching to one side, threatening
to spill out a man covered in blood from his neck to
his groin. A nurse was frantically trying to hold an
oxygen mask to the man's face and keep a blood-
soaked bandage jammed to his chest but the mask was
slipping off and blood was squirting up in a crimson
arc. I jumped in and took the mask from her hands.

"Hold it tight on his face," the nurse yelled, "and
I'll keep pressure on this wound. We have to move
him quick."

I managed to get the mask over the man's mouth
as we swung the gurney through the clinic doors. We
were rushing down a hall, voices shouting, motion a
blur. I used all the concentration I could summon to

keep the mask tight on the man's face and stay up with the speeding stretcher. We turned a quick corner into a small emergency room and the nurse began roughly cutting the man's shirt from him, still struggling to hold the bandage across the man's chest. She glanced up at me. "You okay?"

"I'm okay."

The woman peeled back the bandage and blood gushed up like the stream of a garden hose from a long, jagged tear across the man's chest. I flinched backward but the nurse didn't even seem to notice the blood raining down on her as she probed with her hands through the gore to find the source of the gusher. It was odd but in the midst of all the blood, I kept focusing on the stubble on the man's chin, wondering why he hadn't shaved that morning.

The nurse found the ruptured artery and sealed it off with a long stainless steel clamp. The bloody stream fell away and the nurse swabbed at the man's chest with a thick roll of bandages.

The woman asked if I was okay again and I gave a clumsy thumbs-up. She gestured with her finger toward the ceiling and said "chopper" and I realized I could hear the sounds of a helicopter engine growing somewhere overhead. The nurse told me to hold on and we moved the gurney back down the hallway and then we were rushing the stretcher across a field toward a helicopter with its skids in the mud and its rotors turning. Steady hands took the oxygen mask from me as the stretcher disappeared into a basket in the chopper's belly. Instructions were shouted, doors slammed, the turbine engine screamed into high revs and the chopper lifted its tail and nose-pushed forward, clawing into the air. Suddenly it was gone and silence settled over us like the quiet after a thunderclap. I felt my knees go weak.

Bowen materialized beside me. "How are you, partner?"

"Okay, Nate." I took a breath and scanned the far-off line of mountain ridges to the north. The helicopter was already a dot disappearing into the sky.

The nurse came walking slowing across the muddy field. The front of her tunic and her hands and arms, even her face, were matted in drying blood. She fumbled in a deep pocket and brought out a pack of cigarettes, offering them to me and Bowen. We shook our heads as she lit one up, exhaling a long stream of smoke with an audible sigh. The white cigarette looked alien and awkward in her bloody fingers. "Thanks for the help, stranger," she said. "I didn't have enough hands to get that all done in there."

"Not a problem." I tried to make it sound casual. "Got a bit of blood on you."

The woman let off with a tired laugh. "You should see yourself."

I looked down: the front of my shirt was soaked in blood. I ran a hand over my face and felt it caked on there as well.

The nurse took me by the arm. "Come on. We'll clean you up. Clean both of us up."

Back inside the clinic, she showed me a shower and an examination room and found me a green surgical shirt. As I cleaned up, her voice from the hallway told me to get dressed and have a cup of coffee with her in the office at the end of the hall.

The woman was sitting behind a metal desk peering into the screen of a small computer. Her bloody clothes had been exchanged for a blue blazer over a white cotton blouse and her face and hands had been scrubbed shiny. She looked up as I knocked on the door. "Feeling better?"

"Feeling fine," I said, taking a seat across from her. The woman was handsome in an unpretentious sort of way—probably about my age, light chocolate skin and thick black hair showing the first reluctant strands of grey. She wore only a small touch of makeup on her cheeks and made no effort at all to disguise the tiny wrinkles that had begun to gather at the corners of her eyes.

"Today's festivities?" I asked, glancing toward the computer.

She nodded and her dark eyes turned hard. "There are some very ugly people in the world. The guy you helped works in the lumber mill. He was cutting a log and hit a spike. The saw went off like a bomb. Third episode we've had. I've been searching the Net—trying to find these creeps."

I felt my own face tighten in anger. In their neurotic efforts to stop logging in the Western forests, militant environmentalists had taken to driving steel spikes into standing timber. Mill workers cutting into the wood had no warning they were playing with death: a spinning saw blade hitting a steel spike would explode like an artillery shell, spreading chunks of hot metal through anything nearby. Usually what was nearby was some hapless mill worker whose deepest political concern was putting three squares a day on his family's table. "How's the guy doing?"

"He'll live. It's going to be a while before he can work again. But he'll live." The woman abruptly turned away. An almost imperceptible movement in her shoulders told me she was crying. After a moment she reached behind her and fumbled for a tissue. I handed one over her shoulder. "Sorry," she said, holding her face toward the window, "but it gets to me after a while. People killing people to save trees. Trees! Have we all lost our collective minds?"

After a while she turned around and pulled a cigarette from a drawer, lighting it with a quick motion and settling back to blow a coarse stream of smoke toward the ceiling. "I know," she said, "a doctor smoking a cigarette. Go figure."

"You're the doctor?" I asked, surprised—and realized too late that in the middle of the chaos I'd jumped to a male conclusion: men are doctors, women are nurses, so the woman I helped was a nurse. I felt like a moron, and could tell she'd read my thoughts. "Sorry," I said. "Stupid mistake on my part. I apologize."

"Apology accepted, and thank you. I'm Patricia Hornick. Patients call me Doctor. You should call me Pat." Her drawn smile was tired around the edges.

"Ben Tripp and I'm pleased to meet you."

"And I'm pleased for the help you gave us out there," she said. "Lucky you happened by. You always ride in like the Lone Ranger?"

I shrugged it off. "In the neighborhood and all that. Actually Doctor—Pat—I was planning to drop by anyway. They said up at the Sunshine that the doctor doubles as the coroner. I didn't know it was you, obviously, but I needed to talk to the coroner."

She nodded. "So talk."

"Carson Woolsey?"

"Bad." A single word but a face that implied much more. Frustration, maybe? Anger? I couldn't be sure.

"You did the autopsy?"

"He froze to death," she said. "Why the question?"

"Trying to help a friend."

"That has to be the boy Mike. He's the only one in town who doesn't think Carson died accidentally. You're some sort of investigator?"

"The boy's an old friend. I said I'd see what I could do."

Hornick scanned my face as though looking for clues and seemed to accept what she found there. "Carson froze to death in his truck. It looks to me like he lost control of it in the blizzard, slid off the road, got a good blow to the head that knocked him out and he froze to death before he came to. I could give you the scientific words for all that but it would mean the same thing. He froze to death. I appreciate the boy's concern. I suppose I'd do the same if it were my grandfather. But I have to tell you, his suspicions just don't hold up."

"He wasn't dead first? I mean, he wasn't dead before the body froze? Like somebody killed him and then rolled the truck down into the ditch?"

Another drag on the cigarette before she roughly stubbed it out. "I know Mike thinks somebody killed his grandfather but he was most definitely alive after the knock on the head. And it was most definitely the cold that killed him. Classic symptoms of mortal hypothermia. I've treated a lot of hypothermia over the years in Montana. It's hard to miss."

"The bump on the head?"

"When the truck rolled. I suspect he got it from the doorjamb, maybe the steering wheel."

"So no suspicions in your mind? Nothing strange?"

"Nothing particularly," said Hornick.

"Any chat around town about it? Anything strange?"

The woman let off with a bitter half-laugh and the wrinkles around her eyes seemed to deepen. "Well, let's see. One story has it he was off to meet aliens who'd landed in the Anaconda wilderness. That's pretty good. The little green men thing. And there's the militia. Big green men. He was about to tell their secrets so they executed him. Or maybe it was the environmentalists." Her face turned hard. "This place is sick, if you haven't noticed. Sicker than a simple country doctor can fix."

I doubted she was just a simple country doctor but let it slide. "I'll probably be down and around these parts a bit," I said, getting up. "Maybe we'll meet again?"

Patricia Hornick followed me to the door and extended her hand. "I'd like that," she said. "Maybe next time not so much blood."

FIVE

I FOUND BOWEN sitting on a bench in front of the sheriff's office eating a donut. "Late lunch, partner?" he said, offering the bag in my general direction. "How's the guy?"

"He'll live."

"And how's the doctor?"

"Boy, I got that one wrong," I admitted. "Thought she was a nurse."

Bowen laughed. "So what'd she say about Woolsey?"

"That he died accidentally."

"Maybe he did."

"Maybe," I said. "Where'd you disappear to?"

"Ran a few traps while you were working on your medical degree. What you said about the militia back there in the bar got me wondering so I visited a few guys I do business with, guys who run shops down here." He wiped at his mouth with a paper napkin that looked about the size of a postage stamp in his big hand. "Feels like they've got a pretty big unit working down here—lots of meetings and drills. But nothing connecting them up with Woolsey."

"How big?"

"Hard to say. Maybe a couple dozen guys. They're pretty careful talking about it. Even some of the guys

I know pretty well won't say much. Afraid the feds will come down on 'em.''

"Maybe there's a reason."

Bowen gave me a dubious look and we went in to see the sheriff.

He turned out to be younger than I'd expected—early 30s—and all business, showing us into a map-lined conference room and coming quickly to the point. "I know Mike Woolsey's suspicious," he said in a voice as creased as his nylon trousers. "He thinks somebody killed his grandfather. We think he's wrong." The sheriff let his glance fall purposefully on the two of us. "Cold weather killed his grandfather."

"I appreciate that," I said, slowly. "The coroner agrees with you. And I can't say we don't at this point. But just for argument's sake, did the old man have any real enemies, the kind who'd like to see him dead?"

"Not much there," said the sheriff, resting his right hand on top of his holstered pistol. It looked like a pose he'd spent a lot of time getting just right. "We ran through the people in the community, people he knows—or knew—and came up blank. Talked to the neighbors, though there aren't that many out there. Nothing there."

"What about militia?"

The sheriff straightened and ran a hand over the back of his neck. "It doesn't connect with Carson Woolsey at all. Why the question?"

"A guy whispered it to me." I sensed a wariness in the man that hadn't been there a minute before. "Problems with it?"

The sheriff seemed to choose his words carefully. "We've got some people around who appear to have formed a militia. I deal with them from time to time. I haven't seen them do anything illegal. I'd arrest them if I did.''

''I'm not suggesting you wouldn't. I'm just asking if there's any connection between them and Carson Woolsey?''

The sheriff shook his head. ''None.''

''A fellow told me there'd been some strangers through town.''

''That highway outside the door starts in Alaska and ends in South America. We get a few strangers in town.''

''Anything with the old man's son Edward, Mike's father?''

''We've talked with Ed,'' said the sheriff. ''He and the old man weren't close. Back to when Ed joined the service. He got injured in basic training and came home with an honorable discharge. After that he and the old man were never close. I don't know why that is and I've never asked—it's their business. But Ed's as clear as everyone else on this thing as far as we can tell. They read the will out a couple of days ago. Ed inherits, but that's not a surprise. We checked bank records. There's nothing there. The old boy had a few debts but nothing major. No big piles of money sitting around.''

''Anything with the vehicle?''

''As clean as can be expected,'' said the sheriff. ''No sign of a hit and run, if that's what you're asking. Some damage from when it rolled, windows broken, frame bent. But no paint scrapes like it was hit—and no body damage beyond what you'd expect.''

''Personal stuff?''

''The usual. Wallet, pocket knife, some loose

change. We found a couple of blankets and a burlap sack in the cab. But they could have been there for years. Also a thermos of frozen coffee.''

"Coffee?"

"It was a cold day—not that unusual." The sheriff moved to the back of his chair as though it were a podium. "Let me be as level with you men as I can. We've looked up and down. We've investigated the accident scene, we've looked at the physical evidence. I was there for the autopsy. I've talked to the people he knew. There's nothing out there to suggest that Carson Woolsey died of anything but an accident."

I moved across the room to a large framed wall map of the county. "My friend tells me the ranch is pretty isolated?"

The sheriff nodded and pointed to a small dot circled in black grease pencil. "Sula Basin, twenty, twenty-five miles south of here. Couple of other ranches around but that's about it." He indicated another circled spot along a thin black line of a highway or county road. "We found his car here, about four miles from the house along this road."

I traced the line from the ranch along the road to the spot where Woolsey died. Then followed the road until it came to the end at the edge of the mountains. "What's beyond here?"

"Federal wilderness area."

"The road ends?"

"No roads in a federal wilderness."

I traced the line back down to the ranch. "And no other roads branching off this highway he was on?"

"A few farm lanes that run out into fields. A couple of old mining roads but they're pretty well abandoned."

I traced the black line again from the ranch to the spot where Woolsey died. Then on up the road to where it ended in the mountains. Questions formed in my mind. New questions and the first edge of an old feeling—that something is just a little bit off, that all the ends aren't tying up as neatly as they should. I turned to the sheriff. "Let me ask you this. The guy goes from the ranch up the road to this spot. On one of the worst days of the winter. He goes off the road here and dies. Why's he up here?"

There was a pregnant pause as the sheriff backed up a step or two and surveyed the map. "We haven't figured that one out yet." His voice had lost some of its crease.

"STRANGE," I SAID over the engine noise of my old pickup as we headed south out of Pintler to see where Carson Woolsey had died. Bowen glanced across the cab. "Just strange about that cop. That he hadn't thought about where the man might've been going."

Bowen nodded. "Does seem a bit elementary, Watson. A full blizzard blowin' out there and this old guy's driving down a road goin' nowhere. And old Sherlock-the-Sheriff doesn't think to ponder it. Strange."

Twenty or so miles along we turned off on a narrow paved county road that led into Sula Basin. The basin was actually a small valley, maybe five miles long, half as wide, surrounded by pine and fir-covered mountains now a dark black-green against the greying sky. A pasture stream out of its banks from the spring thaw pooled its overflow in shallow puddles across the road. Black angus cattle with muddy withers ranged through stands of newly budded willow.

The Woolsey ranch sat well back from the road on a gentle slope in the lap of the mountains. I pulled the truck up and killed the engine. In front of us, a curtained picture window looked out from the center of a low single-story log farmhouse. Beyond were a scattering of log sheds, a complex of corrals and a tall barn with an aluminum roof that matched exactly the grey of the sky. The corrals were empty and a shed door hung open on one hinge. In the uncommon quiet, the place had about it the feel of desertion, of things left undone.

I tried the front door but it was locked. Shielding the glare with my hands, I peered through the big window but could make out only a table and a few chairs. Around back, a screened kitchen door was locked up tight but I could make out a kitchen table, a coffee pot next to the stove, dishes in a drying rack next to the sink.

The large barn was open but gave away little. We found where the old man had kept his truck: a few cans and wrenches on the raw wood beams along the rough walls, heavy oil stains in the dirt floor.

Back in the truck, we followed the road up the three or four miles to the spot the sheriff had pointed out on the map. Heavy tracks in the mud showed where a truck had been working, probably the tow truck that had retrieved Woolsey. The tracks led into a ravine maybe thirty feet deep.

I squatted down above the tracks. "The old boy's comin' up this road in a storm and goes off the side."

Bowen came up beside me. "Straight and level chunk of road," he said. "I wonder why he went over?"

"Ice, maybe. You can bet the road was pretty bad."

"Straight and level, partner. You ever run off a straight and level patch?"

I walked back and forth across the area a couple of times. Woolsey had been coming up the road from his ranch. Why? What had been his errand on that miserable day? And what in this level patch of road had suddenly thrown him into the ravine? Wind? Black ice? The asphalt and mud offered no answers.

After a while we climbed back in the pickup and headed up the road toward the mountains. About five miles along, it ended abruptly on a high rounded shoulder that offered a view back out over the Sula Basin. A wooden barricade and a sign in Forest Service brown and green announced the beginning of the wilderness area. Like the deserted ranch behind us, the end of the road had a finality about it. Like the last trip of Carson Woolsey.

In the failing afternoon light I let my eyes play slowly across the mountains, down the foothills, and out across the broad flat basin. I could just make out the tip of the old man's barn miles off in the gathering gloom and trace the narrow ribbon of road that snaked past it. A road that led to nowhere. What could the old man have been doing out on such a day? And what was it out there that could have thrown him to his death in a ditch? The arguments that it had all been an accident were eloquent—and persuasive. But a hunch was growing somewhere deep in my bones that those arguments might be wrong.

SIX

I WAS BACK IN Pintler the next morning early and found Ed Woolsey's insurance office a block off the main drag tucked in next to a feedmill. It was no more than the front part of a small house: the picture window facing the street bore a large gold and red insurance company emblem.

A bell chimed weakly and a woman glanced up from her desk as I walked in. Early-50s, maybe a little older, blue-grey hair teased upward on her head, a touch too much makeup. She wore a knit pantsuit, a white blouse, and a hollow look under cautious eyes that I suspected didn't miss much.

"Morning," I said. "Wondering if Ed Woolsey might be around?"

"I'm Mrs. Woolsey," she said but it didn't sound like a boast.

"Pleased to meet you. He around?"

"Next door at the mill. He'll be back in a minute, if you want to wait?"

"Maybe I can find him," I said, backing out the door. The woman followed me out with her eyes.

Next door at the feedmill, a knot of men standing around the sales counter looked up from their foam cups as I walked in. All but one wore the rough clothes of farmers. I nodded toward the group. "Morning. Trying to find Ed Woolsey?"

The one among them not in farm clothes smiled brightly and stepped forward with his hand out. "I'm Ed. How are ya? Good to see ya." His tone was pushy friendly, a tone that implied he'd known me all his life and seeing me was the high point of his day. A politician's tone. I wondered if it was learned or genetic.

"Ben Tripp," I said, shaking the man's hand. "Down from Missoula and wondered if you've got a few minutes? Got a little business."

Ed Woolsey turned to his friends, smiling. "Catch you boys later," he said, steering me casually but determinedly toward the door. He walked with a slight limp and I recalled the sheriff talking about the man coming back from the service injured. "Beautiful spring day coming, hey?" said the man. "Next couple months this is one of the prettiest parts of America." He guided us back through the belled door of the office. The woman looked up from her desk and I caught just the slightest hint of disapproval as her glance washed over Woolsey.

"Louise," said Woolsey, his voice rushing, "like you to meet Ben Tripp here. From Missoula. Ben, the wife Louise. She pretty well runs things around here— I'm just a paperweight. Louise, honey, maybe you could round up a couple of cups of coffee for us gunfighters here, hey?" Smiling at the "gunfighters," he took a seat behind the desk. "Yup, pretty spring day brewing out there, hey? Been down this way before?" A broad smile cut across his face as he laced two hands behind his crew-cut head and leaned back expansively.

"Been through here from time to time," I offered, neutrally. Woolsey was of medium height and powerfully built through the upper body. His short hair had gone mostly grey but the complexion said it had once been red—like his son's. Woolsey's eyes were set a little too deep in his long face and didn't track exactly in unison. His tie had ducks on it and he wore a small American flag pin in his lapel. He straightened up in his chair and picked up a pen, reconfiguring his face from politician-friendly to worried-pal concerned. "Now, Ben, what can I do for you?"

"Investigating your father's death," I said and watched Woolsey's eyes as they flickered through confusion to disappointment.

"For crying out loud," he said, "haven't I been through that enough in the last month? And what are you supposed to be?" His tone was venomous.

"Investigator."

"What kind?"

"Private."

"And working for who?"

"Can't say."

"That jerk kid of mine," said Woolsey bitterly. "So how'd he find you, Mister Tripp?" He emphasized the "mister" with a nasty twang. I let it slide.

"This won't take much of your time," I said, working to keep my voice pleasant. "Just some questions about it. Anything about the death suspicious in your mind?"

"That jerk kid," said Woolsey. "The old man died in a car wreck. Maybe you haven't heard—the old man died in a plain and simple car wreck. The kid's nuts."

"Pretty hard on your boy."

"My business."

"But you inherit the ranch."

"Oh, that's it, huh?" Woolsey's thin smile had no humor in it. "I killed my father so I could inherit a worthless piece of rock? That the question?"

I shrugged.

"Well, I'll tell ya," said Woolsey. "I sure do inherit. Read the will. I get that ranch—and about a million dollars' worth of inheritance tax. Check the books, jack. I'll have to sell the place just to pay off the tax." Woolsey pushed himself up against the top of the desk and limped around to the side. "Tell you what, Mister Investigator from Missoula. Your interview with me is over. Get out."

The man stood there glaring, his fists balled at his sides, as I backed out of the office and made my way to the pickup. He was still standing there as I drove away and I found myself wondering what the world must look like through the eyes of a small-town insurance salesman.

It was coming on noon as I made it back out to the Sula Basin to see if I could find the neighbor the boy had mentioned—Joe Summey. Considering the nature of the country where the man had scrabbled out a living for so many years, I'd figured Joe Summey would be a pure rustic. By the time I got there, I'd worked the picture into a sort of Montanan Cro Magnon hunched shivering in deerskins over a smoky fire. So much for my ability to predict.

Joe Summey opened the door with a friendly look on his face and a palette of oil paints hooked over his left thumb. Well over six feet, he was wide in the frame in the way of a prizefighter but his face showed no signs of the ring. For a man who had to be well into his 70s, his face in fact looked remarkably young—wide and solid, the features finely etched, almost patrician. The only real sign of age was a slight whitening across the irises of his eyes. His grey hair hung down in a ponytail over a crimson velour shirt.

I offered a brief explanation of myself. Summey seemed satisfied and invited me in. "Mind the clutter," he warned. "I'm afraid you've caught me in the middle of things."

The middle of things was happening in the middle of what in most people's homes would be the living room. In this home it was a large open space with pine-log walls and log rafters. At one end an enormous fireplace framed in rounded river rocks was empty today except for ashes: the room's south wall had been cut into broad floor-to-ceiling windows that offered a panoramic view of the valley and the mountains beyond. In the middle of it all on the bare oak floor a large wooden easel held a stretched white canvas. On it were a few faint brown lines and a smudge of deep blue.

"Landscape," Summey offered. "Just getting started."

The brown lines traced out the tops of the mountains across the valley. The patch of blue was very close to the color of the sky outside the windows.

"You're a professional?"

"I guess I am now," he said in a self-dismissing sort of way. "I took it up years ago after my wife died to have something to keep me busy during the winter. It sort of developed." He walked up next to me and surveyed the canvas critically. "This thing's number three in a series of four. Trying to do the seasons. Commission from a gallery in New Mexico. So far

I've managed to do summer and fall. I'm hoping this turns out to be something like spring''—a short friendly laugh—''then I'll create winter and then rest. Leave the creation of man for God.'' He stood back from the easel and set his palette casually on a wooden chair. ''Cup of coffee?'' I nodded and he disappeared down a hall toward the back, emerging with a couple of mugs and gesturing toward a small table at the windows.

Summey didn't waste much time getting to the point: ''So you're trying to figure out what happened to Carson Woolsey?'' His voice was deep and the delivery refined, as though he'd maybe acted Shakespeare somewhere in his long past: the words had about them an eloquence that seemed out of place in this remote part of the world. Summey pulled out a half-smoked cigar and fussed with it to get it going. His hands were heavy, the fingers stained with paint.

''I don't want to sound casual about this,'' he said, blowing out a stream of smoke and settling back in his chair, ''because it's not a casual thing. A man dying's about as serious as things get. I've heard the talk in town—militia this and militia that. You've probably heard the same thing? But I think it was an accident.''

The same thing I'd heard from the sheriff. The same that I'd heard from Ed Woolsey. And from the doctor.

''I've been chewing it over all winter,'' he said. ''Actually since he first disappeared. I figured then he was probably dead.'' Summey's eyes were measuring me full in the face.

''And...?''

''And, I spent a lot of this long winter past running over in my mind everything I know about Carson—his relatives, his ranch, the way he lives, everything—

looking for a reason that would lead someone to kill him.'' Summey paused to relight the stubby cigar before continuing. "I sort of suspected at first he'd been murdered. People like Carson just don't die in a blizzard. They're just too tough. But there's nothing there to make it murder. No financial problems I can see where he might have gotten himself in a bind. The ranch is long since paid off. No enemies to speak of.''

"You knew him a long time?''

Summey sighed at the question. ''A very long time. Forty years, maybe? Doesn't seem that long. And it actually started out in a fight.''

I arched my eyebrows in a question and Summey smiled.

"Right after the war,'' said Summey. "Carson's old man was still running the place back then and Carson is this young guy just back from the Pacific and full of piss and vinegar. He gets this wild hair up his butt that he's going to open new pasture lands up high on the slopes of the mountains—open up the range and bring in more cattle. Beef prices were real good after the war. So Carson goes up there, pulls down a lot of trees, dynamites out the stumps, grades it off and seeds it to grass. But it's so dry up there nothing's growing. Nothing. He waits a year on the weather but everything dies out. The next spring the old boy puts a dam across one of my creeks—one of *my* creeks—and diverts the water out across the new pasture. Well, I'm sort of full of piss and vinegar too''—Summey's rheumy eyes are shining as he tells the story—''and I get real angry. I go up there and dynamite the dam and then the two of us really get into it.'' A soft chuckle. ''We get into a fist fight right there at the blown-up dam. The next day I'm riding fences way up in the mountains and he takes a shot at me with his deer rifle. A shot. So of course I shoot back and pretty soon we've got a regular little range war going. It lasts pretty much all day, until we both run out of bullets—we don't manage to hit anything except maybe a few trees. Anyway, I'm figurin' we'll start again the next day. Problem is the sheriff shows up. He tells us he hears another shot we're both in jail for a long time.''

Summey smiled almost shyly. ''I guess it was about two years later, I'm out stringing fences, again way up on the edge of the mountains—the fence line that separates our two spreads. I'm out there all alone. Hot summer day. And I spot Carson from a long way off, riding my direction. I pull the rifle off the saddle and ease it down next to where I'm working. He rides up and we stare at each other across the fence for a while—I know he can see the gun. He says something about how hot the weather is. I agree. He asks me if I need any help. I say no. But he gets down from his horse and starts helping me build fence. Right there, just like that. We work up there all day together and by sundown we're pretty good friends. That was almost forty years ago. We've been good neighbors since that day.'' Summey's eyes clouded over and he looked away. ''Damn, I'm going to miss that old son of a sidewinder.''

''Tell me about you,'' I said. ''Artist? Gentleman farmer?''

Summey nodded as though he'd expected the question. ''Funny,'' he said, ''but I figured if I was investigating this, one of the first things I'd do is talk to me. Nearest neighbor, most opportunity, that sort of thing. And I've got no alibi. Bad weather and I was home for a week or more.'' Summey stood up and walked to the windows.

"You ask about my circumstances,'' he continued. "I suppose the best description is widowed rancher and something of a dilettante. My wife died some time ago. I raised a boy and a girl. The boy died when he was nineteen. A farm accident.'' He offered the statement without apparent emotion, though his eyes seemed to draw a little deeper into his face. "My daughter is grown and long gone. I'm probably sitting on a couple million dollars' worth of prime Montana land.'' He smiled. "I like it here, though. It's not for sale.''

"Pretty big ranch for a single guy?''

"I hire people to work it,'' said Summey. "Gives me time for other things.'' We both looked at the canvas. "I started painting a couple of years ago,'' he said. "Mostly to stay busy. Then found there's a land-office market for rustic crap like that. Foo-foo crowd in Sante Fe moreless decided to discover me. I've got to admit it gives me a pretty good living.'' A sly grin crept across his face. "Got a little place down there where I go now and then.''

"Did Woolsey have any other feuds, anything like that?''

Summey seemed to ponder the question for a time. "That's his spread there, you can just make it out.'' I followed his gaze through the broad windows and could see probably two miles off the pitched aluminum roof of Woolsey's barn. "No other neighbors around to speak of,'' said Summey. "The next nearest ranch is four, five miles back down the creek toward the main road. And those folks are new—Californians.'' He said the word like it tasted bad. "It's a small community and Carson kept to himself, mostly. I mean, he wasn't the sort of fellow who'd show up with a potluck dinner and help you put up the hay, if that's what you're asking. He left other people alone and liked to be treated that way himself."

"You know much about his family?"

"Some. Carson has one son, Ed. He runs an insurance office in town."

"Met him."

Summey nodded. "He was just a little boy when his dad and I got into it. I don't think he's ever liked me much since then. At least he hasn't tried selling me insurance." Summey smiled at that. "Ed never seemed able to settle down much. He worked at the feed mill and then partnered up in a grocery store but it went bust and he split from the wife. The woman's still around—she works in the cafe there. Ed got married again, widow of a guy who sold real estate."

"Pants suits and sort of nervous?"

Summey smiled. "That's the one. I hardly know her but I hear she pretty much runs Woolsey's insurance business—and runs Ed too. It's clear who wears the pants suit in that family. I guess Ed's probably doing all right, though. Word had it the woman inherited a little bit of money when her husband died. He wasn't that old—killed in a hunting accident. Getting together with Woolsey sure happened quick after the woman buried her first husband. Seemed like an odd coupling at the time but I guess it's working."

Summey rose from the table and walked up to the canvas, running a finger thoughtfully along the brown lines of the mountains. The smile was gone. "I think it's wrong."

"Sorry?"

"The idea that Carson was murdered," he said over his shoulder without turning. "Wrong."

"How so?"

"It doesn't fit." He picked up a long-handled brush and made a few half-hearted strokes. "This is a tough place, Mister Tripp, the kind of place that can kill you. It doesn't need any help with that."

"Kill you?"

"Kill you," said Summey, his voice taking on a hollow tone. "You probably can't believe some of the things these mountains can throw at you. It's not easy. Blizzards...I don't think you could begin to understand the winters in this part of the world. I lost a whole herd in '59, buried in the drifts. It was 59 below." Summey paused for a time before continuing. "A real tough place to live. And it's just waiting there to grab you. One mistake, that's all it takes. Carson drives off into a blizzard and it kills him. Of course it kills him. Nature's that way. She lets you live until it's time to die. Carson's time to die just came along." Summey slid his brush over the canvas, leaving a broad slash of brown across the outline of the mountains and the little patch of blue.

I started to say something but he interrupted me. "You ever paint?"

"Houses."

"Winters," said Summey in a haunted voice. "They're the tough ones. Montana winters. One of them killed my boy." He was staring at the canvas. "It's not like those white things you see in the galleries, those pictures where the snow looks like cotton and there's little wisps of cerulean blue from the chimney and the windows are golden ochre and the lights are all cadmium orange. Nice and cozy. It's not like that." He slowly stroked the brush across the canvas again, leaving another long brown line. "It's cold colors—cobalt ice, alizarin blood, and snow the color of dead frozen bones. Nobody gets it right."

He made another line across the canvas and then turned to me slowly. "But Carson knew those colors. Cobalt blue, alizarin crimson. Bone white. They killed him."

I left Summey to his canvas feeling spooked—and cold—and turned the heater on as I drove the narrow county road again up toward the mountains. A few miles along, the Woolsey spread looked as deserted as it had the day before—the aluminum roof I'd seen from Summey's front windows, the empty doors of the barn, the vacant, staring windows of the main house. On up the road, at the spot where Woolsey had died, the afternoon sun cast fragile shadows among the slender shoots of crab grass pushing up through the cracked edge of the blacktop. Across the fence, a pasture that had lain dormant under heavy snows for four months was beginning to climb out of the mud in hues of soft yellow and delicate green.

I gazed out across the new life and thought about other places I'd been where death had happened: an Armenian town nature had ground to dust in a seismic twitch, a butchered village in central Africa where man and machetes had done nature's work. Like this spot, there's no memory of death in the landscape, and no guilt: the grass grows, the flowers bud out, and nature seems to care nothing at all about the secrets it covers. With no one there to remember him but me, I tipped an imaginary hat to the dead Carson Woolsey and turned back down the road.

SEVEN

THE DAY HAD dropped away to dark by the time I
made it back to Pintler and pulled up to the Sunshine
Bar to get a little food, and maybe some information.
The front was packed with cars and pickups so I an-
gled down the alley next door and found a spot behind
an empty logging truck.

Inside, the place was a blue cloud of cigarette
smoke and the jukebox was belting out some ballad
about John Deere tractors. I leaned against the bar and
ordered a burger and beer. A different bartender from
the day before: a kid of maybe 24, 25, crewcut dark
hair, white short-sleeve shirt rolled up almost to his
shoulders to show off his tattoos: on one arm a snake
twining around his biceps, on the other a double strand
of barbed wire.

"I was in here yesterday," I said as he put the mug
of beer down in front of me. "The guy behind the
bar? Noon or one o'clock. An older guy?"

"Wolfer," said the bartender, barely glancing up.

"Wolfer?"

"Works weekends mostly." The kid moved down
the bar to take more orders and I sipped my beer and
watched the crowd. The place was nearly full with the
same sorts we'd seen the day before: loggers in red
and black wool plaid shirts and a lot of whiskers, a

sprinkling of cowboys and ranch hands in denim and big belt buckles, and a few ordinary folks in regular clothes who in this crowd looked like aliens.

The bartender set the hamburger in front of me.

"Wolfer have a name?" I asked.

"Wolf, I guess," said the kid.

"First name?"

That seemed to stop him for an instant and he actually knitted his forehead as though deep in thought. It was obviously deep water. "Bob, I think." He looked up at me. "Yeah, Bob." He smiled like he'd passed a test.

I finished the hamburger and nursed the beer. The crowd had gotten lively, shouting over the noise of the jukebox and moving around in an edgy, liquored-up mountain mingle. A couple of women came through the door—blue jeans as tight as paint—and you could almost hear the testosterone begin to sizzle. One threw a glance in my direction that was hard to misinterpret but I was tired and had a long drive home. I paid my tab and left.

Outside, the cool night air tasted good and it was dark enough in the alley that I could make out stars. Castor and Pollux. The Pole Star. And then some somebody hit me over the head. Really hit me. I don't think I'm even conscious as my face bounces off the asphalt. I come to when a boot smashes into my stomach and a lightning-gash of pain tears through my gut. I try to curl up in a ball but get kicked again and I try to rise, try to fight through the pain, but the first kicks have been too much and I get another crushing shot to my gut and I drop back into black.

I struggle out of the darkness into consciousness, like a drowning man gasping for air. I gasp for the

light in my eyes and somehow he's still there and like
a nightmare it's happening again and again and now
I'm on my back and he's an Indian in war paint or
he's a tiger now and he's growling and my whole
body's on fire and I hear him snarl something about
staying away from Pintler—then he says it clearly,
stay away or die—and he smashes his boot into me
again and it's like a steel hammer hitting a glass mirror
and my mind goes skittering away in a thousand jagged pieces.

I don't know how long I lay there. My brain was
firing all over the place but not making much sense of
things and I was blacking out or dissolving into weird
hallucinations about some old guy dressed in beads
and feathers doing a Navajo war dance and then I'm
doing the dance too and then he's doing something to
my head—but then I'm in a car and a guy has some
sort of war club in his hand and he keeps kissing it
and looking at me.

I remember being half-dragged into a building and
then I went out again. When I came to the next time
I actually thought I was dead because I was looking
directly into the eyes of an angel. I'm not particularly
religious—have never really bought into the heaven
and hell scenario—but I almost converted right there.
The angel had one of the most beautiful faces I'd ever
seen in my life. Seriously. These wide brown eyes that
seemed to be looking directly into my soul. Smooth,
gentle hands that were pulling the pain right out of my
skin. And a soft delicate mouth that seemed to be
chanting some almost other-worldly melody.

The next time I came around, my mind was beginning to bring itself back together. My head was on fire
and my stomach was raw and cramped but the hallu-

cinations were gone and I could think enough to make out my surroundings: I was on a bed in a white room and somebody had taken my clothes away and wrapped a bandage around my head.

I tried getting up but the pain was too much and then someone was talking to me. "So, Ben the Private Eye." Pat the Doctor was standing over me with a stethoscope in her hand and a worried look on her face. That face—it came swimming up to me from the dreams—it was the same face I'd mistaken for an angel. "How are you feeling?" she asked.

I managed to grunt something like okay and she told me to hold still while she examined me. I wanted to ask her about the angel face and whether she'd been singing to me but I didn't. She probed at my bandaged head and listened to my chest for a few minutes. "It sounds good enough in there, considering," she said and fished another instrument from the pocket of her white tunic. "Try not to blink." She directed a small light into first one eye and then another and then back again and then took my wrist in her fingers. "Substantial concussion and bruising around the ribs, but nothing's broken. Good thing you're built like a horse. The blows you took could have killed a smaller man. How's your head?"

The word "hurts" came out a mumble.

"I bet it does. We'll let you rest and keep an eye on you. If it gets worse we'll move you to Hamilton and get a CAT scan."

I tried to say something but she told me to be quiet and I went down hard. They said later I slept for more than 24 hours. That sounds about right because when I awoke I had about a two-day growth of beard. I felt a lot better, and had a visitor—Bowen. If I'd expected sympathy, I was bound to be disappointed.

"Mornin' Glory." His loud voice sounded a little too cheerful for the circumstances. "So bumped your head, eh?"

I nodded and felt around at the bandage.

"Got to be careful, your age. Body doesn't recover like it used to." He tossed a bag onto the bed. Donuts. "Readin' this magazine article other day. It said head injuries are sneaky, that sometimes you don't even know their full effect for years. You gotta stop running into things."

The donuts tasted all right.

"Drove past your place this morning," said Bowen. "Gave those worthless horses of yours some grain. Checked out that bedroom you're building. Anybody ever tell you you're a good carpenter? Well, they lied." He helped me with a cup of water. "Are you going to talk," he said, "or is this just a one-man show here? How are you?"

I lay back on the thin hospital pillow. The crushing headache was gone, replaced by a dull throb. "Gettin' there, Nate. 'Bout seventy percent, maybe."

"They said you were about twenty percent when they brought you in."

"I don't remember much."

"Remember Sherlock the Sheriff? He's the one brought you in. A couple of guys saw you in the alley, thought you were drunk—or dead. They called Sherlock."

"How'd you hear about it?"

"Guy I know called me."

"Guy you know?"

The door opened and Pat Hornick came in. "So you're back among the living?"

"Catch you later, Slugger," said Bowen, easing his large bulk out of the room.

Pat unrolled her instruments and I held still while she listened and probed. "It sounds pretty good in there," she said, dusting some donut crumbs off the bed, a look of mild disapproval on her face. "Health food, huh? How are you feeling?"

"Okay. And thanks for patching me up, Doc."

"Let's not make a habit of it, okay?" She gave me an appraising look. "You do live in interesting times. What can you remember?"

I hadn't been conscious long enough over the last two days to dwell on it, but now that I thought about it the images came piling on—the explosion of pain across the back of my head, lying on the ground and feeling the boot smashing into my stomach, the guy who was an Indian or a tiger, the car, the man kissing the war club. The snarled warning to stay out of Pintler, the angel. I told her some of it.

"You took a serious blow. Your ribs are pretty badly bruised but not broken. It's the head injury I've been worried about." She started to say something else but the door opened and the sheriff looked into the room.

"Sorry to bother," he said. "Mind if I come in?" The sheriff had his Stetson in his hands, a revolver that looked all-business strapped into his sam brown. He was every bit as creased and starched as the first time we'd met, formal and ill-at-ease. "Mister Tripp, how are you?"

"Feeling better."

"I'm glad to hear it. You were pretty beat-up last time we met."

"I want to thank you for that. I hear you're the one got me in here?" Seeing his face again, part of the dream sequence unfolded: it was the same face that had been kissing the club. I realized now it must have been the sheriff speaking into the mic of his squad car radio.

The sheriff nodded. "What happened?"

I told him what I could recall.

"Did you have any sort of run-in with anybody in the bar before you came out?"

"None. I talked a little with the bartender. Had a hamburger and beer and left. Then, wham."

"No argument that you maybe took outside to settle?"

"None."

"No argument over women, maybe? I hear a couple of attractive women arrived while you were there?"

"Nothing like that. Had a burger and a beer and left."

"Can you identify the guy who attacked you?"

"Nope. It was dark as a grave out there, and I was actually looking up at the stars, believe it or not. It was a clear night and I was trying to pick out constellations and then, wham, a lot more stars." I chuckled at my own feeble attempt at a joke but the sheriff didn't crack a smile.

"Any ideas who might have done it?"

I quickly ran through my mind the people I'd been around for the past couple of days. Not one of them even remotely seemed like the kind who could flatten me like that. "None, sheriff. I can't imagine who'd be mad enough to do it—who'd be big enough to do it.

No fights down here, no grudges. I don't even know anybody around here."

"I understand you know a few people? Ed Woolsey, Joe Summey?" It came out like an accusation.

"And you," I said.

The sheriff nodded at that and seemed to ease up. "I don't expect Summey or Woolsey's the type to do this sort of thing." He put his white card on the bedside table. "I'll file an official report on this. Ask around a bit, see what develops. How do I reach you?"

I gave him Bowen's number: I don't own a phone, and despite years of teasing from Bowen, I don't intend to get one. Life's intrusive enough as it is.

"You might think about making yourself invisible around these parts for a while," the sheriff said. "Somebody down here doesn't like you a lot."

EIGHT

BOWEN TOOK ME BACK to my place that evening. I slept most of the way and didn't argue much when he fed me a couple of scrambled eggs and a shot of whiskey and sent me to bed.

The sun was pushing toward mid-morning the next day before I managed to get up. It was a warm clear day with the good spring smells of evergreens and new flowers in the air. My head still hurt, but not as much. Bowen had either stayed the night or come back early: He was sitting on the edge of a watering trough reading a book in the sun and—predictably—started talking the minute he saw me walking up. "The other thing they say about head injuries is they make you impotent."

"Mornin' to you too, Nathan."

"Not only make you impotent, but make it so you don't even care you're impotent. Memory goes and you forget about it."

I dipped my hands into the freezing cold water of the trough and dashed it across my face and through my hair.

"Your library's a sad thing, by the way," said Bowen, holding up the book he'd been reading.

I squinted at him.

"How to build a sailboat? You're not getting out

enough, partner.'' He made a small drama of throwing the book down. I shrugged.

''I got you a present.'' Bowen gestured with his head and I looked around. My pickup was parked next to his Jeep. ''Got a wrecker service to haul it up here so I wouldn't get stuck being your personal chauffeur for the rest of my life. How you feelin'?''

I felt gingerly at the bump on the back of my head. ''I'll probably live.''

''That lady doc of yours said I should keep about a half eye on you. Could become a career if you're not a bit more careful.''

I cleaned up as Bowen fixed steak and eggs and moved it outside to the old table. We tossed a few extras to a family of chipmunks begging food underneath the pine.

''I worked the phone quite a bit last night,'' said Bowen. ''Seems a bit of a mystery about what happened to you.''

I had a mouthful of food and formed a question with my eyes.

''Nobody seems to know who or why,'' he said. ''You got any ideas?''

I thought about the people I'd talked to. Only Ed Woolsey had gotten nasty but it didn't have the feel about it of something to fight over. I described the conversation to him and told him about the meeting with the painter, Joe Summey.

''Sounds pretty harmless. Anything else about it, about the attack? I mean aside from the fact that it nearly put out your lights?''

''Well, one thing—the guy said if I ever come back to Pintler, I'm dead.''

Bowen looked up in surprise. ''Dead, huh?'' He

mopped up the last of his eggs and pushed his plate back. ''Wish I'd known this last night before all the phone calls.''

''Slipped my mind.''

''Pitiful mind. Friends I talked to seemed to draw a blank. A couple of them had heard there'd been a bar fight but that was about all they knew. And I'm sort of surprised but old Sherlock the Sheriff seems to be on the case. He'd already called most of these guys before I ever got on the phone. Didn't think he was that motivated.''

I threw the last of the toast to the chipmunks and leaned back in my chair. ''So somebody jumps me and says unless I stay away, I'm dead. Right after I start asking questions about a dead rancher. I don't imagine it's much of a leap to figure out that the two tie up somehow.''

Bowen nodded his head, his face serious.

''So I better get back down to Pintler.''

But I didn't. After Bowen left it seemed hard to concentrate. I fussed around, talking to the horses, checking the oil in the pickup, that sort of thing. But it felt like I couldn't hold a thought for more than a minute before it was skipping away and sinking out of sight like a rock on a pond. And by noon I was asleep again.

It was that way for a couple of days: a lack of energy and focus and I found myself sleeping more than I had in years, but mostly during the day. Bowen came by a couple of times with groceries and we'd talk about the ranch, or about his store, sometimes about Pintler and Carson Woolsey, but then I'd have to go down for a nap.

Nights were particularly bad. I'd dream about the

attack, about the sparks of pain in my head, about the man in the tiger face, and I'd wake with a start, sweat-drenched and feeling small and stick-like and frightened that there was somebody there in my dark room waiting for me. Often as not I'd pour myself a water glass full of bourbon and sit there nursing it until the sun came up and I could fall back into a dreamless stupor.

It was after one of those bouts that Pat Hornick showed up. I didn't even hear her drive in. I came awake and she was sitting there watching me. It spooked me—like coming to after the attack with her hovering over me. She seems to come out of nowhere and I'm never ready for it. I pulled the blanket up around my chin and tried to collect myself.

"Morning." Her voice was gentle, her eyes quiet. "How are you feeling?"

"Doc."

"Sorry to drop in without warning," she said in a tone that contained no apology whatsoever, "but I thought it might be worth a house call. Your friend Mister Bowen called me, worried. He said you were either sleeping all the time or not at all."

I swung myself up to sit on the side of the bed, still wrapped in the blanket, and ran my hands through my hair. My head was banging, but it had more to do with whiskey than Pintler. I decided I shouldn't let her know that.

"I knocked on the door," she said, "but I guess you didn't hear me?"

"Sorry. I was under pretty good." I looked down and realized the blanket had come open to show some parts I didn't want shown. I stuffed a fold between my legs.

"Why don't I wait outside," she said.

I threw on some clothes, gobbled a few aspirin and set coffee to brew.

"So, the good doctor," I said, joining her at the table under the pine, trying to trowel a smile onto my face and some cheer into my system. "What brings you to these parts?"

"Down this way and thought I'd pop in." Her lips were on the edge of a smile. "Though I must say, this way is a long way from anywhere."

I nodded. "I don't like crowds. Surprised you could get away. How's life in Pintler?"

"A doctor from Hamilton's covering for me. How's the head?"

"Coming along. At least it doesn't hurt much."

"Dizzy spells?"

"None."

"Memory?"

"Have we met?"

She smiled at that. "Sleeping?"

I gave her about half the truth. "Things seem to be a bit turned around. I do okay during the day, not so well at night."

"Bad dreams?"

"How'd you know?"

"It's the pathology of head wounds. Things get mixed up. Lots of buried things surface. Nightmares are fairly common but they go away after a while. Anything unusual besides that?"

"Should there be?"

Her smile had turned into a sly grin. "I had a patient once, a dairy farmer. A big old brute of a fellow, bald, a nose as big as a turkey baster. I mean, he was ugly." Pat's grin widened. "One of his cows kicked him in

the head and he was out for two days. When he came
to he was convinced he was a ballroom dancer.'' Pat
was giggling. ''I don't think he'd ever danced a step
in his life. Suddenly he's a ballroom dancer...can you
imagine this big old dairy farmer doing the tango?''

We're both chuckling.

''Oh, it's dreadful to laugh at the poor man,'' said
Pat, and then she laughed out loud and covered her
mouth with her hand. ''Oh, that's awful of me. Doctors don't laugh at their patients.''

''Milk barn rehearsals must be quite a sight.''

''I see him around from time to time. He calls himself the Rhumba King of Montana. The ballroom milk-
barn Rhumba King.''

After a while I brought out the coffee. We talked
about the ranch, and Pat talked a little about herself.
Mexican parents—her maiden name had been Gonzales, Patricia Gonzales—but she'd been raised by
Mormons: medical school at Brigham Young in Salt
Lake, an internship at the medical center there and
then a job in private practice.

''You wouldn't know it now,'' she said, ''but as a
little girl I had a severe stammer. So bad I couldn't
talk and my parents kept me out of school. They
wanted to institutionalize me but we didn't have the
money and the state wouldn't do it, so I sat at home.
Until I was ten. A pretty hopeless case.''

''And then?''

''And then the Mormon Church. We weren't even
Mormons. There aren't a lot of Mexican Mormons.
But the church showed up one day and just sort of
took me away. God bless the Mormons. They put me
in a special school where I learned all over again how

to talk. I decided to become a doctor to pay some of that back.''

As she got older, she said, her life was changing and she started looking to move away—like me, looking for a spot off the map. She'd heard of an opening in Pintler and applied, finding out after she got the job that she was the only applicant. It was a tough role to step into: the town didn't like women doctors and cared even less for Mexicans. It had been difficult at first, but the town had gradually warmed to her. It's not like they had a choice.

She'd been married and raised a daughter—studying to be a doctor as well. She didn't talk about her husband and I didn't ask, but it sounded like it was past tense. She'd just bought a house—her eyes lit up like gemstones as she talked about it: not very big but it was on a creek and at night she could hear the water ''talking to the rocks'' as she put it and feel the wind as it came up in the pines. She was thinking about becoming Patricia Gonzales again, now that the town had begun to accept her. It was a matter of working up the nerve.

At length she brought the conversation back toward me. ''So,'' she said, ''who's this Ben Tripp guy who came charging into my life. The Lone Ranger? Something like that?''

I tried shrugging it off but she persisted. ''You certainly jumped in there the other day at the clinic. I don't think most people would be so quick to wade into that kind of bloodbath.'' She crossed her arms over her chest and gave me an openly questioning look. ''And your story, Mister Tripp?''

''Maybe the Tango King of Montana?'' I said, smiling.

She held her gaze steady. "It sounded a little more interesting than that the other day."

"Sorry?"

"When you were out. In the clinic. You talked quite a lot in your sleep."

"I hate that."

She laughed lightly. "Who's Barbara?"

"Oh geez. Ex-wife."

"Figured it must have been something like that. You didn't seem to like her very much."

"What'd I say?"

"Something I can't repeat in polite company."

"I really hate that. What else did I say?"

"What's an AK-47?"

"I talked about that?"

"A lot."

"A Russian assault rifle."

"You were yelling about an AK-47."

"Some guy tried killing me with one once."

Her brown eyes widened. "Tried killing you?"

"Long story. But he missed, sort of. Anything else?"

"I'll spare you the embarrassment, for the moment." Her eyes were shining. "So what is a Ben Tripp?"

"Okay, okay," I said, putting up my hands as though in surrender. "A rancher, a sometimes carpenter, and an occasional private eye."

"I see the ranch and I see the carpentry," she said, nodding toward the bedroom addition. "But I don't see the private eye part. Where's that coming from?"

"A long time back," I said. "I used to work in newspapers. The investigative kind. I tracked down the bad guys."

"Seriously bad guys?"

I nodded "The seriously bad guys."

"Your friend Bowen says you were good."

"I lie to him."

"Good enough for a Pulitzer, is what Bowen said."

"Long time ago on a planet far, far away."

"And he says you got tired of it and quit," said Pat. "True?"

"More or less."

"And came back to Montana?"

"That part's true."

"And that you're real smart and real good?"

"I pay Bowen to say those things around pretty woman."

"Why so skittish?"

"I'm not."

"You are."

"Okay," I answered, feeling mildly exasperated at her persistence. "I grew up in these parts. Son of a rancher, but it wasn't much of a ranch. When I came back from the war the place seemed too small, too claustrophobic, so I got out. Newspapering got me out, actually. I had a knack for it, I guess—the investigative type. Lived on airplanes for a long time. Got married along the way but it didn't last. I covered a lot of dirty little wars, saw lots of dead people—and a lot of stupidity. And after a while I figured out what I was doing was utterly pointless. So I came home." I looked across the table at her. "And so here I am. Taking tango lessons from a pretty woman."

"One day, maybe, we can get below that leathery hide." She fumbled in her purse and pulled out a couple of sheets of paper and some black and white photographs. "When you turned up injured at the clinic,

I realized it had to be connected somehow to what you were doing. I went back through the autopsy, back through my notes. But I still don't see a thing in here. The evidence says he froze to death.''

"Someone helped him."

"How can you say that with such certainty? I know I can't.''

"I couldn't, until the attack in the alley. The guy told me to stay away from Pintler or he'd kill me.''

Pat's eyes widened. "Or he'd kill you?''

I nodded. "That means somebody killed Woolsey. And they're worried enough to do the same to me.''

"Ben, this is serious. You have to take it to the sheriff.''

"He could be part of the problem.''

"He's the sheriff.''

"And somebody's killing people. It's a tight little town. I don't take it to anybody until I get a better lay of the land.''

Pat's face was tight, her eyes worried. "I'm frightened for you, Ben.''

"They had one clear shot," I said. "They won't get another.''

"I can't believe I'm saying this but do you carry a gun?''

I shook my head.

"Maybe you better.''

"Guns come out and people have a way of getting shot. I had enough guns in the war.''

"But…''

"I don't need a gun, Pat. Trust me.''

"I want to help.''

I shook my head. "It's a proven fact now that it's a dangerous pursuit.''

"And I'm a tough woman. I've been that way for forty-some years. Where do I start?"

"I can't let you."

"Actually, you can't stop me," she said, her face defiant. "I don't like murder in my little town."

"You'd have to be careful."

"I live that way."

"We find the guy, he could go to the gas chamber. He's probably willing to do pretty much anything to avoid that."

"There's no gas chamber in Montana, Ben. We hang them here. And I don't have a problem with that. Now tell me what you know about Carson Woolsey."

NINE

"GET LOST!" The words came at me like a shot from behind the closed metal door.

I banged on it hard with my fist. "Three minutes!" I yelled back, feeling the anger build up inside me. I generally try to give my fellow man a break but this guy was wearing me out. Not only had I ignored a seriously ugly warning to stay out of Pintler, but now I'd spent an entire morning tracking the bartender Bob Wolf to this dingy trailer park on the edge of town. I didn't intend to waste it. "You said 'militia.' That needs explaining."

Silence for a moment from behind the door and then: "Bad topic in these parts. And there's some people out there don't like you much as it is. Go away."

So that was it. Word that someone had tried to crush my head had obviously put a chill on things. "We've got to talk."

"Go away."

I gave the door one final shot with my fist and the whole trailer trembled. "Fine. Either we talk here, just the two of us—or I talk real loud in the bar in front of all your pals. Your choice."

A hesitation and then: "Not here."

"Where?"

"Not here," said the voice from behind the door, "and not daylight."

I named a motel on the highway north of town. "I'll be there tonight. Grey pickup at the door."

"Maybe," said the muffled voice. "Now get lost."

I drove away from the run-down trailer park feeling like a hundred eyes had to be watching me from behind the sooty windows—and wondering if paranoia was a communicable disease.

Pintler didn't seem quite as quaint as it had before the night in the alley. It felt now like enemy territory, a place where I had to soften my step and watch my back.

The local cafe where the former Mrs. Woolsey worked was busy with the late lunch crowd. I shoehorned myself onto a stool at the counter between a thin man in a dark suit and a farmer who hadn't bothered to take his cap off to eat. Two waitresses were handling the crush of diners and another woman was seating people and ringing up tabs. I tried guessing which might be Ed's ex. One waitress seemed a little young and a little too much on the make: there was an edge to her like she'd never been married. The other two women were both middle-aged, both a little plain. I had a hunch that the woman working the counter was probably it—something in her eyes seemed tired and a little out of focus, fixed at a point about halfway between angry and hopeless. I ordered the special—the roast-beef sandwich and mashed potatoes—and watched the locals.

Small-town cafes can tell you a lot about a place. This one said times were pretty good. Towns struggling to make it don't have restaurants this busy, and the people around me looked prosperous—a good mix of new clothes and shined shoes, a few bright colors here and there and a lot of briefcases. From what I knew about western Montana, it was a pretty good bet most of those briefcases were carrying real estate brochures: land prices all over the state were booming as every Hollywood star and wannabe crowded in to buy their little piece of the honest-to-god authentic cowboy West and establish bragging rights on the Mulholland cocktail circuit. It's funny, but before all this cheap tinsel started showing up, most of the farmers and ranchers could barely afford to go to the movies. Now they were shoving piles of new cash in their pockets— and moving to California. It seemed to me California was getting the better end of the deal.

I finished my lunch and sat over coffee as the crowd began to thin. The woman behind the counter was in her late 40s, brown hair as tired as her face, chapped hands that worked for a living. "Ma'am?" I said. "Got a minute?"

"More coffee?" She was friendly enough—just hurried, businesslike.

"Ed Woolsey?" I said.

She shot a wary glance across my face. My hunch about her had been right.

"Trying to get some information," I said.

"You're a friend of his?"

I took an easy gamble: "Not in the least. You?"

"Grab a booth and I'll be there in a minute."

It was more like half an hour before the woman brought over her own cup of coffee and slid into the booth across from me. She made a small production of lighting a cigarette and then slumped back against the fake leather cushion. "So you're not a friend of his?" she said. "That's a good start."

"Investigator," I said. "Ben Tripp. Checking into the circumstances surrounding Carson Woolsey's death."

She didn't seem surprised. "Grandpa, huh?" The woman took a heavy drag and blew out a tight stream of smoke. "Poor old guy. Actually, I take that back: I hope he rots in hell. What's this about?"

I went through it for her: how I'd been investigating what some people were suspecting wasn't an accidental death, how I'd talked to a few people who knew him. I didn't mention the attack in the alley.

"You talk to my ex-husband?" she asked.

"Not long. He found out I wasn't buying insurance and didn't have much time for me."

She answered with a bitter smile. "That's Ed. He'd probably be a pretty good crook if he was half smart, but he isn't. So what do you want from me?"

"Information… I'm trying to get enough to build a picture of who the man was and how it came to be that he wasn't anymore."

"And you think somebody killed him?"

"Other people think so. I'm trying to find out if they're right."

"I guess I'm probably sorry he died," said the woman. "Not that I cared much for the old guy, but he was pretty good to my boy. Have you talked with Mike?"

I nodded. "Nice kid."

Her tired face seemed to light up at that. "Yeah, he's a good boy. He's always been a good boy. It's been tough for him, though. When Ed and I divorced, Mike gravitated toward his grandpa. Me working and all, there just wasn't as much time to give him and he started getting closer to Carson."

"But you didn't like the old man?"

"Not really."

"Reasons?"

She tasted her coffee and took some time before answering. "Tough times during the divorce. We were yanking back and forth on property and who's going to get Mike. Old Carson sided with Ed—grandfather and father against me. They wanted to take my boy away from me. Carson got real nasty. I called him every name in the Yellow Pages. I ended up getting Mike but it was a bad fight. And it left bad feelings. Mine especially."

"When did you and Ed divorce?"

"Ed divorced me."

"Sorry."

"There's a difference." She stubbed out her cigarette and quickly fired up another. "He divorced me, and it was seven years ago next month. I thought at first it was me, you know, like something about me was bad. He comes home one day and announces he's rented an apartment and he's moving out. Right out of the blue. He says he's out of here, see ya. It hit me like an atom bomb. A young boy to feed and take care of, house payments to make. He'd even hired a lawyer. Then I find out he's already in the saddle with another woman. I should've guessed it. A real piece of work, that woman. The stories I've heard."

"Such as?"

"Such as check into how her first husband died. Hunting accident, hah! She killed him. Plain as a prom pimple she killed him. Then waved her cash and Ed came running, zipper open and tongue out."

"I met her. She seemed almost timid."

The former Mrs. Woolsey snorted out a mean laugh. "That woman timid? And I'm the Pope."

"Was she ever charged?"

"She bought 'em off is what she did. Bought 'em off and skated away waving her bundle and Ed came after her like a shark. Hope they're happy. Two sharks doin' it." Deep bitterness in her crooked smile and her eyes seemed to be somewhere else.

"Carson Woolsey," I said. "Do you know of anybody ever threatening him, anybody who'd want to kill him?"

The woman brought her eyes back to the conversation. "No's the simple answer. I suppose some people liked him, a lot didn't. But there's nothing out there at the killing level."

"A lot of people didn't like him?"

"Business, mostly, I guess. The old guy had a ruthless streak in 'em a mile wide." The woman shot a worried look around the room. "I've gotta get back to the counter."

"But who didn't like him?"

She was gathering up her cigarettes and edging toward the end of the booth. "It's not that kind of dislike. It was the small stuff like he'd get rude if he got overcharged for groceries, gas, that sort of thing. Nasty to his neighbors. I do have to get back to work. Sorry."

I sat there for a few minutes playing with my cold coffee and wondering if it was worth hanging around to get a few more words with her. I'd found out little: a nasty divorce and a custody fight. No surprises there. Ed-the-Insurance-Salesman had maybe managed to remarry into some money. I knew that already. The new Mrs. Woolsey? More of a question mark than I'd thought—maybe. What had the painter/rancher Summey said about her? Who wears the pants suit in that family? And Carson Woolsey wasn't quite the saint he'd been painted. Who is? I settled up my bill and headed back up the highway to keep a date with a bartender.

The Shamrock Motel had seen better days, but they weren't recent. I'd gone on up to Hamilton to buy a few provisions for the night and pulled into the Shamrock just as the sun was going down. The room was post-war, barely: a narrow sagging bed with an orange spread, brown deep-pile carpeting, a wooden chair and a small desk edged with cigarette burns. An ancient television was bolted to the cabinet and the black phone was the kind without a dial that hooked directly to the main desk.

I locked the door and checked the window. The darkened parking lot was almost empty. Stowing a new book and a sixpack of beer on the desk, I tried calling Hornick. The receptionist told me she was with a patient and I left her the name and number of the motel. The TV didn't work but the book did—a detailed history of food that opened with a nice line about how a Connecticut Yankee in King Arthur's Court would have starved to death because the English liked their food so rotten it would have made a modern Yankee sick. Before long I was actually enjoying myself in a perverse sort of way, like I was on vacation or something. The phone rang a couple of hours in.

"Slap and Tickle," I answered.

A long pause on the other end and then Pat's uncertain voice: "What?"

"Sorry," I said, grinning into the phone.

"Ben?"

"Hi Doc."

"What'd you call it?"

"Stupid joke. How are you?"

"You're in a motel?"

"A long story. How's business?"

"Why a motel?"

"Beats sleeping in my truck."

"Are you drunk?"

"One beer. Honest, doctor. Actually, I'm waiting to meet a guy." I told her about the reluctant bartender. She said it might be dangerous. I told her I didn't think it was and actually got her to laugh describing the scuzzy room.

"I have a little bit of news." She said it almost shyly.

"Yeah?"

"Yeah. I called a realtor friend of mine today to see if there'd been anything happening with the Woolsey ranch."

"And?"

"And, I stumbled across something that might be interesting. There's no movement now but there was a big flurry on it four years ago."

"A flurry?"

"A flurry, is what my friend called it. Carson Woolsey put the ranch on the market about four years ago. He did a contract with a realtor in Hamilton. They showed it for a couple of weeks and there was lots of interest because it's prime land. Every realtor in western Montana was trying to get a piece of the action. But then he pulled it off."

"Pulled it off?"

"Pulled it off the market."

"They say why?"

"No. They just closed the books on it. One day it's for sale, the next day it isn't."

"Maybe they made a secret deal, something like that?"

"It doesn't look like it," she said. "My friend went through the property rolls on her computer. The place is still listed in the name Carson Woolsey. The will has been read and it's in probate: Ed Woolsey inherits the place. So it's staying in the family. No secret sale."

As she was talking, a car pulled into the lot outside my window and doused its lights.

"I think I've got company," I said into the phone. "Bartender?"

"I'll call you." I cradled the phone and cracked open the door. A wedge of light spilled out into the courtyard, about half-illuminating the figure of a man sitting behind the wheel. I offered a flat-handed wave and the man killed the engine and got out, looking around in the darkness.

"Wolf?" I said as he brushed past me into the room. The man was as I remembered him from the bar: a stocky fellow with a large gut, thin black hair pulled back from his forehead, a waxy complexion on a nervous face.

I offered Wolf the wooden chair and a warm beer, which he took cautiously. "You brought up the militia the other day," I said. "I need to talk about that."

His voice was tight. "Anybody know I'm here?"

"Nobody."

"I carry a gun, you know."

I'd noticed the bulge on his waist. "I don't," I said.

"This meeting never happened, okay?"

I nodded. "Never happened. So tell me about the militia."

"I wanna be clear on this," he said. "I'm not in it. You're a federal agent, you've got nothing on me. And the gun's licensed."

"I'm not an agent," I answered, "and whether you're in it or not doesn't mean anything at all to me. Clear enough?"

The man nodded and seemed to relax slightly. "What do you want to know?"

"How it ties into Woolsey."

"I didn't say it did."

"You said if I wanted to know about Woolsey, I should ask about the militia. I'm asking."

Wolf seemed careful about the words he used. "I don't know anything firsthand, all right? Just stuff I pick up at the bar." I nodded. "Those guys are nuts," he said. "I mean really nuts. I hear 'em talking about taking back the government, organizing coups, stuff like that."

"I've read about it."

He snorted. "Reading and hearing's two different things. These people are lunatics. I heard a couple of 'em talking about killing a senator because he'd voted for gun controls. I mean, these people are really psycho."

"So how's it tie to Woolsey?"

"They hated Woolsey, too."

"Why?"

"Who knows. Maybe they just don't like him or maybe the old guy did 'em, jabbed 'em over something."

"Jabbed 'em?"

"Double-crossed them, something like that."

"Was Woolsey in the militia?"

"Not that I ever heard."

"Then what's it about?"

"I never found out. But it's been that way for a while, a couple of years at least. I'd hear snatches of conversations, you know. I mean it's not like these people are my pals. I'd just hear things that made it pretty clear they didn't like old Woolsey, among others."

"But you never heard why?"

"Never."

I thought about the militia not liking people—and absently rubbed the knot across the back of my head. "You hear anything about the attack on me?"

"Bar fight's all I heard."

"Hear who did it?"

Wolf shook his head and took a drink.

"You think it was militia?"

"Heard it was a bar fight. Word I got is you eyed the wrong woman."

My mind flashed on the two women who'd entered the bar just as I was getting ready to leave. One of them had shot me an unmistakable look. Too brief, though—too innocent. Nothing worth fighting over. "Word's wrong," I said. "It was some other agenda. You said there'd been strangers around?"

Wolf nodded. "See 'em from time to time."

"In the bar?"

"Yeah."

"What do you mean strangers?"

"Strangers," he said, "like in people I don't know. But they're not just passin' through. That's a different type."

"Men?"

He nodded.

"Businessmen, something like that?"

"Rougher than that."

"Rougher?"

"Like workers or something. They're in work clothes."

"How many?"

"Well, they're strangers, so I don't know."

"But two or three?"

"Probably."

"Doing what?"

"Nothing. I mean, how do I know, huh? I'm just telling you I've seen some people around town who don't live there."

"Militia?"

"Maybe, maybe not."

"You think they're connected to Woolsey?"

He shook his head. "No way of knowing."

"Anything specific on Woolsey? What's the word on him dying?"

"Speculation, mostly."

"What sort of speculation?"

"Mostly militia—that they took him out for some reason. Yeah, I'd say mostly militia."

"But why would they take him out? Seems to me it's a pretty reckless thing to do. Reasons?"

Wolf shook his head. "No reasons that I've heard. I know there's bad blood—I've heard them talking about it. And there's some people who think the militia's behind it. But I can't give you reasons."

"Who're the militia players?"

"Whoa." Wolf put both hands up like I was attacking him. "I may be top-ten dumb, but I'm not the dumbest."

"What's your problem?"

"I'll have enough problems they hear I was talking to you. Not going to finger 'em too. Just not." Wolf stood up.

"Easy there," I said, standing with him. "I'm not aiming to get you in trouble. But I need to know where to look."

"Under rocks," said Wolf and he was out the door and gone.

I watched his car make a quick turn out of the lot and disappear into the darkness, then double-locked the door and popped my own beer, running the encounter back through my head. Wolf didn't have anything. There's militia around. Big deal. There's militia all over Montana. Maybe they didn't like Woolsey. Sounds like a lot of people didn't like Woolsey. There are strangers in town. So what? It's a strange town. Wolf was nervous. Maybe he had reason to be. Or maybe he was worried that I'd figure out he was just another small-town gossip who couldn't quite catch the difference between rumor and fact.

It had been a long day of talking, and I couldn't see that it had accomplished much. After years of it you get a feel for how a search is going—and this one was feeling empty to me. Talk to enough people, you should start to get hints and directions. I'd talked to plenty but so far had little to show for it. Doubts, confusion—yes, plenty or it. But actual hard information that gave me a direction? The only thing solid I had was a bump on the back of my head and a couple of sore ribs.

I must have fallen asleep because the next thing I knew somebody was at the door. I fumbled my way up out of a groggy fog in a small panic—a motel in

Pintler was not a place to let my guard down. I unlocked the door and cautiously edged it open. Pat Hornick was standing there in her white physician's lab coat with a worried look on her face. "You okay?" she asked in a loud whisper.

I pushed the door open, offering an exaggerated bow. "Kinda late for house calls?"

Her look of concern washed to irritation as she walked into the room. "I got worried when you hung up on me," she said. "Why'd you do that?"

I thought she was joking. "Sorry. I had a visitor."

She wasn't. "I don't like getting hung up on," she said. "You've already been beaten almost to death once and now you're in some god-awful motel room..." She stopped herself in mid-sentence and turned in a slow circle, a small off-center smile growing on her lips. "It really is god-awful, isn't it?"

"Not so bad," I said. "You ought to see where I live."

"I have," she said dryly. "You okay?"

"The guy came and went. Routine."

"Anything?"

"Not much." I told her about Wolf and the gun in his waist, his suspicions—and his absolute lack of any sort of hard evidence.

"So where are we?" she said, leaning back against the desk. Her light brown face and chocolate eyes seemed to glow in the dim light and I thought about the angel I'd met as I came to after the alley. Not a hard mistake to make. Maybe it was the hour, maybe it was something about the forced intimacy of the small room, but her breath created an almost hypnotic swell across her chest, and even the casual act of running her long fingers absently through her black hair seemed erotic. I found myself mentally unwrapping her from the white lab coat, separating out the human being from under the formidable trappings of a physician.

I opened a warm beer and handed it to her. "You really look great tonight."

She took a self-conscious sip from the can. "Your phone call scared me."

"Sorry about that."

She was quiet for a minute and then: "I'm talking to you on the phone and then some guy is showing up and I don't know who he is. And you're all alone. I got worried that you'd get hurt."

"I'm careful."

"I saw the scars of how careful you are." She offered the comment with a neutral expression on her face.

"Sorry?"

"Your scars. I saw them when I was cleaning you up after the alley."

My cheeks reddened as I realized she must have had a better view of me naked than I'd ever had. "Old holes."

"Bullet holes, if I'm any kind of coroner."

I tried shrugging it off.

"Too new for the war," she said. "Where'd they come from?"

"Bullets, mostly." I was the only one who smiled. "A couple of different places, none all that romantic."

"Lone Rangering?"

"Hardly."

"Then where?"

"You are nosy, aren't you? I got one from a misguided professor up in Missoula. It's a long story but he was a little nuts.''

"Was?"

"Dead now.'' I didn't add that he'd tried killing me with a prehistoric bone—and that I'd gotten him first. "The other one's courtesy of a man in Somalia. We had a slight disagreement.''

"Disagreement?"

"He wanted to shoot me and I didn't want to get shot.''

"Your AK-47 dreams?"

"Probably.''

Pat set the beer down and crossed her arms on her chest. "I was frightened for you,'' she said in a soft, tentative voice. "That's a new feeling for me.''

Something in the way she was standing there so vulnerably, something about the night, about the mood, something made me feel like I should wrap her in my arms and feel her chest against mine and whisper to her that it was all right, that everything would be fine. It was close. It was a heartbeat away and I don't know what held me back, but I didn't. "There's nothing to be frightened of,'' I said. Maybe in my mind I hadn't managed to strip off the doctor's white smock—or maybe it was the honest truth that I didn't know it was all right, that everything would be fine.

She seemed to read my thoughts. For about a breath and a half, we looked into each other's eyes. I could have held the gaze through the night, but Pat broke it off.

"I have to go,'' she said. "There's a pregnant lady waiting.'' Her tone was a doctor's again. But it was clear to me the relationship had changed.

I walked her the couple of steps to the door. "You eat dinner?"

She smiled. "Some days."

"This day, maybe?"

She shook her head. "Pregnant lady."

"Tomorrow then?"

Pat smiled. "Depends on the pregnant lady."

"I'll call you?"

Pat nodded. "Stay safe Ben." With that she kissed me softly on the cheek and hurried to her car.

I stood there watching as she pulled out of the lot and disappeared into the darkness. Pintler was becoming a strange place for me—dangerous, and seductive.

TEN

THE NEXT MORNING I was out of the motel early and on the road south toward the Woolsey ranch. It was a cold, wet morning of heavy clouds lying low on the mountains, drizzle against the windshield, cattle up under the trees—a morning of grey sky and brown mud. My mood paralleled the weather, and I wore out the rearview mirror checking for unwanted company.

Woolsey's place seemed even more lifeless than before. The sightless windows of the main house reflected back vacantly in coffee-colored puddles of rainwater across the gravel driveway. The barn sat empty and silent in the soft rain, its main doors hanging open forlornly. The place had about it an almost desperate air of abandonment, the feeling that it was slowly dying for want of a hand to put things back in order, to give it some life.

I stopped at the head of the lane to check if anyone might have been following and then parked the pickup out of sight behind the barn and began working my way methodically through the place where Carson Woolsey had lived his life.

The barn edged onto a corral and a pair of smaller buildings. One turned out to be a granary. Empty, mostly, except for some old wheat and barley kernels scattered here and there on the dusty floor. A cured ham wrapped in a rough burlap sack hung from the rafters in one corner. I spun it slowly and the rope creaked eerily in the silence.

The building next door was long and squat with an almost flat roof and two large doors that swung open on solid iron hinges. Inside in the dim light I could make out heavy farm equipment: a large red and grey tractor with oversized double tires on the rear axle, a heavy five-bottomed plow, and a few other smaller pieces of equipment parked in ordered neatness and precision in the silent gloom. I thought of what people had said about Woolsey being a very careful man.

Next door, the big barn was split into two separate areas. The larger of the two was where Woolsey had kept his truck, the place Bowen and I had visited the first day—a dry earth floor stained with grease and oil, a few oil cans on the rough wood beams along the walls, a spare tire, and a couple of old six-volt batteries.

The other side was a milking parlor that had been turned into a work shop. One end seemed to be a sort of tack room: two shiny leather saddles straddled wooden saw horses. At the other end, an old anvil was bolted to a shop table, next to it an electric whetstone and grinder, boxes of nails and bolts, more containers of screws and pipe fittings, staples, washers, clamps, hoses. Ordered clutter throughout, like a iron snapshot of a man's life—and it was beginning to spook me a little, looking through his gear. Tools are a personal thing. Good tools become like friends, almost like members of the family, and if you're the kind of man who cares about things like family, you care about your tools. Now, snooping through Woolsey's, I had the feeling that I was somehow intruding, nosing into the very private. It was one thing talking to Woolsey's kin: they could take care of themselves. But the tools were defenseless to my prying, and innocent in his death. I closed the barn doors and walked up to the house.

The back door was locked but I managed to force it open with my pocketknife and let myself in. Somebody had been busy since I looked through the windows a week or more before. The kitchen shelves and cupboards had been emptied and cardboard boxes lay along the countertop and on the table packed and sealed. The next room, the living room, had been about half packed—more boxes stacked here and there but whoever was packing hadn't gotten all the way through. An ornate Seth Thomas clock sat silently on the mantel over the fireplace, its hands frozen at a little after four. On one wall a cabinet still held a couple of shelves of books—mysteries, mostly, along with a stack of news magazines, something called the Rancher's Companion, a book on gems and mineralogy, and a Bible. I cracked open the Bible's cover. "On the birth of Carson Milright Woolsey January 11, 1917," it said in a tight scrawl of sepia ink, "May God In Justice give you long life. Mother." He had. I set the Bible back carefully on the shelf.

The house was almost eerily quiet as I made my way through. Dust and faded wallpaper in one bedroom suggested it had been empty long before Woolsey died. The other had a bare mattress on a wooden frame, a small nightstand with a yellowed alarm clock and a wooden lamp carved in the shape of an owl. I sorted through the cabinet's single drawer: two worn pocketknives, a jeweler's loupe on a white shoe string, an old slide rule in a plastic sleeve, a few coins. Everything else was empty or had been packed up. If there ever had been something in that house to tell me the story of Carson Woolsey's death, it was gone now.

Back outside, the clouds were beginning to lift and I could make out the foothills that rose gently beyond the pasture. They were still grey-brown in the early spring, dotted here and there with patches of dark green juniper. A narrow tractor path led up across the face of the first foothill, disappearing from view into the low clouds. About halfway up the hillside the ruts seemed to be darker and I guessed a spring or something cut through the path at that point.

An invariable rule of the game is listen to your instincts. Most of the time they're the only thing you have. And my instincts, for whatever reason, told me something was a bit off on that hillside. It was a feeble message—no more than one or two errant neurons firing out of sequence. But I was getting to that desperate point where I'd pay attention to anything if it had even the most remote chance of paying off. I started up the pickup to find out what was on that hill.

The hard-packed rock and gravel trail led out through an open gate beyond the corrals and across probably a quarter of a mile of overgrown pasture before edging upward. I put the truck in low and moved on slowly. About midway up, I came on the darker area I'd seen from below. As I'd guessed, it was a small spring which seeped from a rock ledge and trickled across the road, pooling in a couple of moss-covered puddles in the ruts. And in those ruts I could make out fresh tire tracks. They looked like they were probably made by a truck or some sort of off-road vehicle. Each was about a foot wide with heavy, deep treads and they couldn't have been more than a few days old. There was nothing jarringly obvious about them, just a pair of tire tracks in the mud. Maybe some hunter had been up this path, or maybe a Woolsey had been checking out the ranch. But where they were—on the ranch of a dead man—and when they had been made—well after he died—were enough to make me want to find out what might be at the top of that hill.

I climbed back in the pickup and followed the road as it climbed upward from the spring. Clouds closed in and I couldn't see for more than about a hundred yards. At the top the hill flattened out into a mesa or butte and the road cut along a wall of fir trees. After another mile or so it opened into a small meadow.

I killed the engine and eased myself cautiously out of the cab. Something had obviously been going on here.

The ground all around was churned up with the heavy tracks of a bulldozer. A number of small trees and saplings had been broken off and lay in the debris. Scattered over the area in a regular grid-like pattern I could make out small piles of earth and broken rock, each probably two or three feet high—about half a dozen of them all together. It was almost as though someone had marked out a football field by stacking up rocks at regular intervals around the edges. But this was no football field.

Another part of the meadow looked like it had been scalped. It was about half the size of the first area and had been scraped clean of brush and topsoil down a couple of feet to a layer of rust-colored rock. Just beyond that, someone had dug a trench maybe twenty feet wide, five or ten feet deep. Gravel and rock was piled up next to it. Nearby, signs of an old campfire.

By the look of the new grass coming up and the

way things had been weathered down by the elements, I figured the work had gone on maybe six months, even a year before. It was hard to be any more precise. But it was obvious it had been carried out before Woolsey died.

I made my way down into the trench. The walls and the floor were the same rust-colored rock that I'd seen all around. In the very bottom of the trench someone had dug a rough pit maybe a yard wide and a yard deep. This work seemed to be newer, like whoever had excavated the larger trench had come in much later and dug out the small pit.

Near the newer hole, something yellow was peeking up from amid the rocks. I scuffed at it with my boot and uncovered a tattered piece of paper about the size of my hand. On it in heavy black print were the letters "HA". The rest of the word had been ripped away. I stuck it in my pocket and walked back and forth across the area a couple of times but there was nothing else to give away what might have been going on.

Back in the pickup, I pulled out the scrap of paper and stared at it for some time, trying to divine what it might be. Yellow, jagged and torn around the edges, the letters "HA" on it. Nothing in and of itself that offered anything. But that I'd found it on Woolsey's ranch in the middle of some odd unexplained activity meant that maybe, just maybe, it might be connected somehow to an old man dead in a ditch.

I sat for a while surveying the scene, trying to put together what I'd found. Someone with heavy equipment had come up here last summer or fall and attacked this small meadow for some reason. They'd turned over the soil and pushed a lot of dirt around but there were no obvious signs to say what they'd been doing. Then they'd come back again, maybe a few weeks or maybe even just a few days ago, and dug another hole, again for a reason I couldn't begin to imagine. I wondered if the tracks I'd found back down the road at the spring had been made by the people who'd dug that newer hole.

Sitting there and looking at the red earth, I couldn't put a name to it, or a label, but the bruised meadow seemed to have an edgy, disturbed feeling about it. Maybe it was just me: too much time in Pintler, too much pain and paranoia. But up there on that dead-silent stretch of lonely mountain, the small patch of mauled earth felt off-center and off-key. Did it somehow know about the murder of an old man? Had it played a part?

I came off the mountain feeling tight and edgy myself. And things got even tighter on the way back to Pintler when I decided I had gotten myself a tail. Whoever it was—if it really was somebody—stayed well back and I couldn't even make out a car for sure. It was more of a feeling than an actual presence—a flash in the rearview mirror a couple of times—but it was enough to make my hands sweat and the skin on the back of my neck crawl. I pulled over outside Pintler and called Pat from a phone booth, watching the traffic as it swirled past. Nothing obvious. Maybe it was only nerves. I willed myself to calm down.

For a change, Pat was in.

"How's the pregnant lady from last night?" I asked.

"Pregnant no more," said Pat, her voice husky with fatigue. "An all-nighter but a bouncing baby girl. Mom's fine. Dad's a mess. The doctor's worn out. How's the detective business?"

"Interesting."

"Really?"

"Dinner?"

A short pause on the line and then: "I've been up since yesterday."

"Life's never easy."

"I look a mess."

"Not possible."

"I might drown in my soup."

"I have a lifeguard certificate."

"Figures."

WE MET EARLY EVENING at a place halfway between her town and mine, a new restaurant catering to the newly landed gentry buying up the big spreads along the edge of the mountains. Linen on the tables, venison on the menu, and a wine cellar the size of an ICBM missile silo.

Pat was at a candle-lit table near the windows, looking out at the blue farm lights that shone here and there like small lonely sentinels posted off across the rolling foothills. She turned smiling as I sat down. "Hey cowboy. Glad you could make it."

Maybe I'd seen her too many times in the white lab coat, but the way she looked tonight took my breath away: an elegant black outfit and a small emerald pendant that dangled above the low-cut edge of a gold satin blouse, black hair glinting like quicksilver in the soft light and a sheen of ruby gloss across lips that were bending into a gently teasing smile. The edgy meadow and the creeping paranoia were instantly forgotten.

"And the good doctor?" I said. "Where'd you leave her tonight?"

The smile deepened. "I decided I'd give her the night off and let her evil twin out for a change."

"Your evil twin is stunning."

"And you look pretty good, too, cowboy. Thank you."

"Nice outfit."

Pat looked down across her chest with a self-appraising glance and then brought her eyes back up to mine. "I think I don't get out of the lab coat as much as I should. Funny about that sort of thing."

"What sort of thing?"

The waiter hovered and I ordered wine.

"It's just funny in a sick sort of way," she said. "You work all your life to get somewhere, and by the time you get there it's the only thing you know how to do." The smile was dying away. "I don't think I said that well. What I mean is, you get so intent on doing one thing well you don't let anything else into your life. That make any sense?"

"I think I know what you mean."

The waiter arrived and poured the wine with some ceremony.

"You know probably better than most, don't you?" said Pat. "You turned your back on it completely, didn't you?"

I nodded. "It took a long time for that to happen."

"But it happened."

"It happened."

"And it hasn't happened to me." Pat took a sip of wine and put the glass down gently on the linen tablecloth. "It was strange tonight—getting dressed up. I can't tell you the last time I dressed to go to dinner. It was fun. I mean it's kind of fun being a woman."

She said it almost shyly, as though she was looking for my approval.

"You're very good at it."

"I don't do it much. I don't do anything. Dammit."

I took her hands into mine and smiled. "You settle down a bit, Ms. Gonzales. You look great. And we'll do this some more. Get both of us out of our ruts a bit."

The smile came back. "You fish a lot, don't you?"

"Fish?"

She laughed. "Fish. Infinitive form: to fish. Yeah, fish. Your friend Nathan said you fish a lot."

"Do I fish a lot?"

The laugh again. "Hello Ben. My name's Pat and I have a question from the audience. Do you fish a lot?"

"Some."

"Worms?"

"Worms? I can't believe I'm sitting in this place with a beautiful woman talking about worms."

"Worms or flies?"

"God, you're persistent."

"You fly fish, right?" Her teasing smile again. "I mean, real men fly fish, right?"

"Okay, I fly fish."

"A lot?"

"What's a lot?"

"Once a week?"

"Maybe once a month."

"So once a month you go fishing?"

"You a game warden?"

"I'm a doctor. So you go fishing a dozen times a year?"

"Well, it's probably more than that when you put it that way."

"I've never been fishing."

"How can someone never have been fishing?"

"I haven't."

"What do you do then?"

"Nothing. I'm a doctor."

"You don't do anything?"

Pat shook her head. "Teach me to fly fish sometime?"

"In that outfit?"

The waiter interrupted. "Doctor Hornick?"

Pat looked up and the laughter died.

"There's a phone call for you," said the man.

"Not tonight," said Pat, folding her napkin and leaving the table. When she returned her face was narrow and her eyes tired. "I'm sorry, Ben, but my new baby's not doing well. I have to go. I'm sorry."

I paid the abbreviated check and walked her outside to her car.

"It was almost a lovely evening," said Pat, clenching her hands into fists at her side. "I'm sorry."

I unknotted her hands and held them in mine. "It's all right. Let's consider it a training round. Next time the real thing." I bent to kiss her cheek but she turned her face into mine and briefly met my lips with hers.

She turned and climbed into her car. "We'll do it again?"

I nodded. "Next time."

"Next time," she said and drove away.

ELEVEN

THE TROUBLE WITH this kind of work is its frustrating insistence on not being predictable. I like predictability: like to know when the sun's going to come up and go down, when the seasons will change and the fish will bite, that sort of thing. I organize and build schedules in my mind to fight the lack of predictability. When things are organized, they're manageable, predictable. Life's easier. That's why I'd never do this sort of thing full-time. It's not that it's too dangerous—it's just too unpredictable.

A case in point: after the day prowling around Woolsey's ranch punctuated by the almost-dinner with Pat, I had a notion things would move along briskly. I had a big hole in the ground, a piece of yellow paper, and somebody maybe actually shadowing me. Not unreasonable to assume things had a good chance of moving along. The problem was, they didn't.

By the time I got back to the ranch late that night after the abbreviated dinner, the sense that I had a tail had vanished and there was no sign that anyone had been nosing around. I checked through the house and around the barn but I was alone. I never lock the door but that night I did, and then spent a glass of whiskey looking at the yellow paper and thinking about Carson Woolsey's torn-up meadow. No answers.

The next morning I drove down to Bowen's store to use his phone and show him the scrap of yellow paper with the HA on it. He was busy sorting through a computer catalogue and hardly paid any attention. I tried calling Mike Woolsey but the people at the grocery store said he wasn't around. Ed Woolsey wouldn't take my call. Frustrated, I took the scrap of yellow paper to the county sheriff in Missoula who drew as big a blank as Bowen, promised he'd talk to some of his deputies but I probably shouldn't hold my breath. I even dropped in on the big research library at the university where they acted like I'd just landed from Mars. It's funny how places like that can be: real good at figuring out four thousand-year-old Indian burial mounds, and not worth a whistle in dealing with the here and now. My final try was a construction firm out west of town near the airport. I reasoned that if someone with heavy equipment had been up there moving earth around, a construction firm would likely know what was going on. The owner called in the foreman and together they listened to my description and studied the scrap of paper. They talked about it quite a while—it might be a trench for a foundation but probably not, maybe an irrigation scheme but it didn't sound like it, possibly a quarry of some sort but they didn't know much about that kind of operation. They said they'd ask around.

I went back to the cabin and basically sulked for a while, hoping that some of the asking-around might pay off but realizing that after two weeks on the case, all I had to show for it was an occasional headache, a lingering sense of paranoia, and a scrap of yellow paper with a couple of letters on it.

The weather was good so I mostly worked on the

bedroom. I finished framing it out and managed to get in the big window that would give me the view out over the pasture toward the mountains. I went to town to get a load of plaster board for the interior walls... and the answer I'd been knocking myself out to find was sitting there in the window of a hardware store. I slammed on the brakes and swerved into a parking spot, nearly wrecking the pickup and managing to scare a few years off a metermaid. Under a sign that said "New Lawns Deserve the Very Best" they'd piled up a pyramid of HAWKIN'S fertilizer bags. Yellow bags. HA—WKIN'S. No mistaking it: the same color paper, the same printing as the HA scrap I'd been carrying around. Fertilizer. Scientific for cow manure.

I sat there and stared at it for a while, swinging from small triumph to minor despair: it was nice to have finally figured out the clue—it made me feel almost like an honest-to-God detective. But what I'd found was frustratingly insignificant: a bag of fertilizer on a ranch is about as unusual as a fence post, and just about as revealing. I anted up two and a half bucks, loaded a bag of it in the back, and headed for Bowen's, figuring I could brag a little about my masterly discovery—and hoping maybe he'd have some clue about what exactly it was that I'd discovered.

Bowen had an actual customer, a guy shopping for a .22 rifle, so I unloaded the bag onto his back porch table and waited. I heard the cash register ring after a while and he came out, irritated.

"Brought you a present, Nate."

"Bag of manure, huh? Anniversary?"

"Fertilizer."

"That guy took more than an hour in there."

"It has the letters HA on it. Same as the scrap I found up in the hills."

Bowen seemed to be looking at the bag, but it was obvious his mind was somewhere else. "Couldn't make up his mind."

"It means they had this fertilizer up there above Woolsey's where they were digging around. That's where I found the scrap of paper. What do you think?"

"Then the old fart wanted a senior's discount. I took five percent off just to get him out of the store. I tell you, Ben, sometimes I cannot stand my fellow man."

"Why do you s'pose they'd have fertilizer up there? That's pasture up there. You don't fertilize pasture."

"Guy's probably going to end up shooting his foot off." Bowen settled heavily in his ragged easy chair and seemed to focus for the first time on the yellow sack sitting there. "Hawkin's fertilizer, huh? Same stuff you found up there?"

I nodded. Sometimes it wasn't worth explaining.

He pulled a pair of reading glasses from his breast pocket and studied the label for a time, then took them off and leaned back in his chair. "Explosives, partner."

The words went through me like an electric shock. "What?"

"Explosives. Read the label. Basic ingredient's ammonium nitrate. Good enough fertilizer. Mix it with diesel, excellent explosive. Same thing that guy used to blow up the federal building. Remember? Truckload of ammonium nitrate and diesel?"

"That hadn't occurred to me," I said lamely. My brain had gotten locked on fertilizer as a farm tool and hadn't allowed for any other creative thoughts to edge in.

A serious look had grown on Bowen's face. "They're either growin' or blowin' up there, Ben. It's gotta be one of the two."

I flashed back across the scene in the high meadow: the ground all torn up with heavy tracks, the soil stripped off to the rock below, the big trench. And now possibly something else going on up there. "It makes a pretty good explosive, huh?"

"One of the best," said Bowen. "Cheap, easy to make. Everybody's using it."

"Everybody like who? The militia?"

"I mean that generally," said Bowen, cautiously.

"Your friends?"

A rare sharp glance of irritation. "Not my friends, Ben. I know people who know them but they're not my friends."

"But you said if it's not growin', it's blowin'. Nobody's growing anything up there where I found this."

"Then somebody's blowing something, partner."

"I need an introduction to the militia, Nate."

"They're a paranoid crowd."

"Maybe we'd better figure out if they have something to be paranoid about."

Bowen looked at me long and hard. "I'll see what I can do."

I used Bowen's phone to make more calls to Pintler. The sheriff wasn't in and I left a message. No luck either with the bartender Wolf. I finally reached Mike Woolsey. He didn't know about the fertilizer and didn't know about the torn-up meadow either. But he did have one item that he'd overlooked when we talked at the bar: a few years earlier his grandfather had gotten tired of trying to keep the ranch up and had rented parts of it out to a corporate ranch, an outfit called Westlands. He had a Missoula phone number for it.

I finally tracked the Westlands, Inc. people to a massive field ten or so miles out of town. A couple of new white pickups with Westlands signs on the doors were parked on the edge of the field. Two men and a dazzling young woman were leaning against the fenders sharing a thermos and watching probably three dozen people with hoes weeding and clearing beds that would soon be planted to sugar beets. Migrant labor—Mexicans mostly, among them a scattering of women and, illegally, a few children. The law said they were supposed to be in school but it was a law most people ignored as the families moved with the crops and the seasons across the northwest. I admired the migrants: my best friend as a kid had been the son of the son of a migrant who washed up in Montana. He'd scratched out a good farm and a decent life and just never went home. As an illegal, he was always afraid of the government even though his sons fought in two wars.

The Westlanders gestured me over. The two men looked like field workers themselves in jeans, blue cotton shirts, and heavy boots. The woman was in jeans and boots, too. But you could tell that unlike the men, she'd designer-dressed down for the trip out to the fields—expensive bleached jeans that hugged her supple form like a second skin and a simple white blouse with sleeves rolled to the elbows and open in the front to show off significant cleavage. She reminded me of one of those catwalk models in the grocery store magazines. The woman had a narrow waist, flaring hips, blond hair cut a little above the shoulders and quick eyes in a tanned face. Smooth hands with long fingers and red nails, no wedding ring. I thought briefly of Pat Hornick in her doctor's smock, wondering how she'd look in the same white blouse and tight jeans there in front of me. Introductions all around and it was only the woman's name I got: Roberta Feldy. Friends called her Bobby, she told me in a husky voice, she was the boss, ran the Missoula office of Westlands, and how could she help.

I explained myself up to a point, sketching in the concerns over Carson Woolsey's death and trying to keep my eyes from wandering too often to her chest.

"We were shocked," she said. "Such a nice man. We'd been dealing with him for years and years. I'm new—I just came in last year—but the company's been there for the last five or six years. I don't know what'll happen now." She told the two men to check the next field over and turned back to me, concern in her blue eyes: "It's the first I've heard of any suspicions about Mr. Woolsey's death. We thought he'd died in a car wreck."

"It's a concern among some of his relatives," I said, "that maybe the accident wasn't all that accidental."

"I'm truly shocked. Let me tell you Westlands will do anything—everything—it can to help. You tell me what you need."

"Information," I said. "What your deal was with Woolsey. What kind of work you do there. That sort of thing."

"Ranching, basically," said Roberta. "It's the same kind of deal we have with most of the big spreads. We rent out parts of the land and the livestock, run the place and share profits with the owner. We eat the losses ourselves, basically. I'm afraid I can't be specific about the actual financial deal, you understand?''

I nodded. ''You do any improvements on the land? New construction, irrigation canals, things like that?''

She formed a question with her eyes. ''Not usually. We do general upkeep on fences that are already there, barns and sheds, things like that, but nothing new. We don't build things, if that's your question. There's new construction?''

''A few miles back from the house. It looked like construction of some sort.''

''Buildings, something like that?''

''A meadow, actually, that had been torn up. Some trenching too.''

''I'll have to check it,'' she said, ''but I haven't heard about anything.''

''A friend of mine said he'd once in a while hear shooting back on the property. Anything unusual like that?''

''Nothing I ever heard about.'' A questioning look on her face. ''What kind of shooting?''

''I don't know. Maybe target practice.''

She shook her head.

''Also,'' I said, ''I found the remains of a fertilizer sack up there. Does that ring a bell of any sort?''

''Spring planting?'' she offered.

''It didn't look like planting to me. And it's not crop land up there, just mountains, pasture.''

''I know we've been doing spring work on the ranch. Maybe it's part of it.''

I thought of the tire tracks I'd come across in the puddles. ''Anybody else have access up there? Are you partnered up with anyone, something like that? I guess what I mean is would someone else have business up there besides you—legitimate business?''

She seemed to chew over the question briefly before answering. ''Well, I suppose people could get on there if they wanted to. It's not like you can lock up a ranch. But, no, we're not in partnership with anyone on the place. Maybe it's the family?''

I shrugged. ''I'll check it. But nothing unusual on the place, nothing out of the ordinary?''

A look of concern washed through her eyes. ''Nothing I've heard but they keep me pretty much bound to a desk up here. I'll check with my people.''

I gave her Bowen's number and she promised to let me know what she found out.

I was almost home when my truck started ringing. I'll try that again. I'd driven most of the way back up to my ranch when something in the pickup started making this strange, insistent ringing noise. My mind, as usual, instantly assumed the worst and I figured I'd either thrown a piston or had a bomb about to go off under the seat. I pulled off to the side of the road in a panic and killed the engine. Worse than a bomb: I had a mobile phone in my glove box. I pawed at it and held it up to my ear uncertainly.

''You there?'' said a tinny voice from within.

I held the phone out and looked at it as though that might help. ''Who's this?''

The tinny voice again. ''What hath God wrought?''

''Bowen?'' I said. ''That you?''

''Livingston?''

''Bowen? That's you isn't it? Bowen, for crying out loud?''

The voice on the other end collapsed into laughter.

"Bowen, you moron, you scared me half to death. I thought the truck was about to explode."

More laughter, Bowen trying to catch his breath. "Easy, Ben old boy. You thought the truck was exploding?" and he lapsed off again into waves of laughter. I sat there holding the phone to my ear, looking about as adequate as a squirrel with a guitar. It was a while before Bowen collected himself enough to talk, though he was still having troubles with his air supply. "Phew, that was funny. I can just see you sitting there in that old truck with that phone. That's great."

"What's with this thing?"

"I know how you like 'em," said Bowen. "So I thought I'd loan you one for a while." Deep laughter still hit the surface in waves of chuckles out of the little black box.

"What am I supposed to do with this thing?"

"Snuck it into your truck," he said. "The charger and a manual are under the seat. Number's on a piece of tape on the side."

"I don't like these things."

"Figured the number of calls I'm getting for you, you'd better take my phone for a while. I'm gettin' worn out arranging your social schedule."

"I got some calls?"

"Doctor friend of yours. Sheriff friend of yours. Friend friend of yours. I lose track."

"Messages?"

"Ben, you are a pure frustration. What do you think they said? Write them letters? Call them back, genius. You ever make any money being a detective?" He hung up laughing and I went on up the road feeling like somebody had slipped a snake in my lunch box.

TWELVE

AFTER A WHILE I used the phone—grudgingly. I suppose they have a place in society. It's just that I'd gotten sick of them: more than twenty years on the road and always a phone to my ear. It wasn't so bad in the early days before cell phones. Back then you could actually be out of touch—really get lost—and people couldn't find you. Now, though, everyone's got these precious little things. I even saw a guy fly fishing with one held up to his head. He should've been shot.

Anyway, I used Bowen's cellphone. Pat Hornick didn't have much to say, had just been checking in to make sure I was okay.

"Great dinner, by the way," she said and I could hear a smile under her voice.

"I particularly liked the pheasant," I said.

"And the lamb with rosemary was superb."

"Dessert wore me out."

Pat laughing: "I warned you. Brandy and port don't mix."

"I think it was the champagne. Cleared the palate nicely, though. Next time I think I'll try the jellied eel."

"Ick," said Pat. "Just the name sounds horrid."

"Big favorite in London. Eel pies, too."

"That's gross."

"And potted dormouse."

"What?"

"Potted dormouse. The English used to love them. They'd take this little mouse, see, and can it in a jar of honey. Two or three months later...appetizers."

"Gross."

"Speaking of little potted things, how's that kid who interrupted our evening?"

"Recovered," said Pat. "Mom managed to feed him some spoiled formula. One bad night but everything's okay now."

"And how's Pat the doctor?"

"Recovering, too," she said. "How are things going?"

"Moving along," I said and told her about figuring out the scrap of paper, about the visit to Westlands. I didn't tell her about the woman with blond hair and big aspirations. We hung up promising each other dinner.

It was the middle of the night when the new phone started ringing. I fumbled around in the dark and got it to my ear as a woman's voice was saying, "Come on, Big Bone, wake up. You said you were going to call me. You awake? Huh?"

Big Bone? "Hello," I said.

Instant uncertainty on the other end and a tentative "hello?"

"Hello?" I said back. We were beginning to sound like a couple of answering machines mating.

"Nathan?" Her voice pinching now toward uncertainty.

"Ben Tripp," I said.

"What have you done with him?"

"Who?"

"Is he all right?" Impatience was beginning to shade out the uncertainty.

"Is who all right?"

"Nathan. Is he there? And who's this?"

"Nathan Bowen?"

"I know Nathan Bowen," she said curtly, "and you're not Nathan Bowen." The line went dead in my ear. I waited maybe thirty seconds in the dark before it rang again. I was grinning by then: I said hello and the line went dead. No more calls and I put myself to sleep laughing silently at the mileage I'd get out of casually calling Bowen "Big Bone" in the middle of his morning paper. Big Bone. Maybe make him faint.

It was probably three in the morning when I came around again. I don't know what it was exactly, but I came awake frightened: something was going on outside in the darkness. Memories of the attack in the alley fresh in my head, I slid noiselessly from the bed and crept naked across the darkened room, trying to keep my breathing low and silent. I edged my face up next to the window frame and peered out. A quarter moon was just setting. The barnyard seemed deserted and the driveway looked empty. I could just make out the three horses on the far edge of the dark pasture. Two were grazing but the third had her head up and seemed to be looking toward the house, toward me.

I noiselessly slipped a filleting knife with a long thin blade from the block by the sink. Holding it ready out in front of me, I padded across the room to the front door and eased it back a crack, wedging my face around the side and scanning out. Cold night air came pushing through. I opened it further, swinging it out slowly and silently. Still nothing. I moved outside. Eerie shadows in the near-darkness. Then, a soft sound, like a stifled breath from around the side of the house. A razor-wire bolt of adrenaline shot through my system. I wouldn't be taken by surprise this time. I edged on tiptoe toward the corner of the house, my back up against the wooden siding, my senses straining for every sound or movement. I came to the corner and flattened, waiting. Heavy darkness, unnatural stillness. I made myself count silently to ten, gathering my energy, judging my prey. Another almost inaudible breath or grunt. I lunged around the corner, screaming in the darkness and slashing out with my knife.

And probably came as close as any human being ever has to giving a black bear a heart attack. The animal was on all fours nosing into an old tulip bed. When I came around the corner all at once, screaming and naked, it must have seemed to the creature like some vision of bear hell. Its eyes wild in terror, the bear rolled back onto its hind legs with a sort of high-pitched shriek, tumbled all the way over onto its back, and then did a mad scramble to get its feet under it and run like a terrified fat dog toward the trees, looking back over its shoulder with wild eyes at the human who'd scared it almost to death.

I stood there for a moment panting, naked, amazed—the adrenaline still buzzing through my system—when my eyes caught a brief flash of light off in the distance. I stopped, the bear forgotten, and watched the distant darkened forest. There, another flash. Dim white light bouncing off a green wall of pine trees maybe a half mile away. Headlights. A car driving back down off the mountain. Someone had been up there, up there at three in the morning on a road that leads only to me. Someone had been up there and had turned around. I wasn't alone.

I waited in the darkness for probably five minutes before the chill forced me back inside. No more lights but no sleep that night.

The morning finally came and I lost myself in work. I was covered head-to-toe in plaster dust when the phone rang again.

A woman's voice again, familiar: "Ben?"

I thought it was the same woman from the night before who'd been looking for Big Bone. At least she had my name right this time. "Yup." I managed to put just the hint of a snigger into the single word.

"Roberta Feldy from Westlands. Morning."

Oops. Wrong woman. I wondered if she'd heard the leer in my voice. "Mornin' Roberta. And how's life down on the corporate farm?"

"Just fine, Ben." At least I could hear a smile in her voice. "The reason I'm calling, I talked to some of my people about the Woolsey property. Do you eat lunch?"

I did a quick survey around me: lunch would mean stopping work, cleaning up, and driving all the way into town again. I thought about the quick eyes and ample chest and heard myself name a pricey restaurant down by the river.

I was squeezing lemon into an ice tea when Roberta made her entrance, and made heads turn. She'd poured herself into tight black slacks under a black blazer, a fire-engine-red blouse that wasn't meant to hide her chest, and a pair of high heels that made her look seven feet tall. She gave me an air-kiss on the cheek like we were neighbors in Malibu or something.

Small-talk for a while: today was an in-the-office day for her so no boots or blue jeans. I complimented her outfit. She asked about me and I told her some of it. She seemed to be in a touchy mood: almost every time she'd say something, she'd touch my hand or arm for emphasis. I thought it was quaint at first. Then it got to be distracting—it seemed a little too intimate for the setting and I started paying more attention to that than to what we were talking about, trying to guess when the long fingers would brush across my skin.

We managed idle chat through salads as she took me through her career: daughter of a small-claim silver miner in Idaho, school in Oregon, the career trail with Westlands. This was her first job actually running things on her own and it was a challenge, as she put it. She touched my knuckles to emphasize the word. It took us most of lunch to get around to Woolsey.

"I've really been thinking over what you said," she offered as she sipped her coffee. "And I can't imagine that someone would mean harm to sweet Carson." She said it as a question and I shrugged. "I met him a couple of times," she continued, "and he seemed like such a gentle, lovely old man. He even made cookies for one of my visits. He had them out on the good china with milk." She touched my hand as she said it and her eyes misted up. I looked away in embarrassment but she collected herself quickly. "Anyway, I checked with our guy who runs things down in the Sula Basin. You mentioned you found some construction up in that meadow? Well, my foreman thinks maybe Woolsey might have been doing something up there. Maybe a stock pond or something? It's not anything we've been doing. He says Woolsey was always fussing around with ponds and damming up creeks, that sort of thing. I asked him to check on it and he said he'd try to get up there in the next week or two, see what's going on." Roberta's eyes formed a tender question. "Does that help? I mean, I know that's one of the things you'd mentioned and I really want to help on this. Problem is, we just don't get up into the high mountains very much. The profit's in the croplands down on the flat—wheat and barley, some hay."

"Let's see what he finds," I said.

"You'd also mentioned shooting up there," said Roberta. "I asked our foreman. That was news to him."

"And the fertilizer?" I said, "the Hawkin's fertilizer?"

She was shaking her head. "He didn't know anything about that. Maybe the wind blew it in?"

The day had turned cloudy. We talked some more— Roberta tried turning the conversation back toward me—but my mood had dropped into a hole. There was also something else niggling at the edges of my consciousness as we sat there. Once or twice when my eyes darted across Roberta's chest, I flashed on a different meal, a different woman sitting across from me: Pat in the candlelight, her black hair flashing, her lips forming into the small teasing smile. A tale of two women: Roberta here confident, self-possessed, glamorous, her whole character worn across her skin like a neon sign. And Pat—quiet, understated, a little uncertain about herself—and somehow mysterious. I suppose it's a stupid male thing but I thought about cars as we sat there waiting for the check. Pat the doctor was a four-door, comfortable, elegant, built for the long road. Maybe not as flashy, not as quick, but sturdy, substantial. Roberta was a sports car, all curves and flash, built for speed. Slick bucket seats you could slide right into, quick on the corners, fast on the straightaways. At dinner a few nights before, the comfortable four-door had seemed just exactly right. Now I wasn't too sure.

I walked Roberta to her car—a sports car—gave her an air-kiss, and sent her on her way with a vague promise that we'd be in touch. I made my own way home less certain than ever about Carson Woolsey, and more confused than usual about women.

THIRTEEN

IT WAS—unmistakably—automatic weapons fire. Small caliber, not much more than .22 or .25, but the signature ta-ta-ta rip of a rifle on full automatic. Like somebody hitting a metal drum with a hammer. A deadly hammer.

Bowen and I exchanged glances and scanned the woods to either side but the heavy brush revealed little. Bowen slowed his green Jeep to a crawl—he'd said when he called the night before with the militia's invitation that his car would spook them less than mine. We moved slowly up the gravel road another quarter of a mile or so before he pulled off onto a wide spot in the trees.

"This is the place," Bowen said, his voice uncharacteristically tense. "They told me eleven miles from the main road. Eleven miles exactly." He killed the engine and the forest seemed to swallow us in a soft rushing stillness. "They said to wait and they'd come to us."

We'd been there maybe five minutes when I heard them. Actually what I heard was a human trying to whistle like a blue jay. But he got it all wrong and instead of a blue jay he sounded precisely like a guy trying to whistle like a blue jay.

I glanced at Bowen and he made a stupid face: he'd

heard it too. So much for the rough and ready militia: if we'd been an enemy patrol, they'd be in body bags. We waited another couple of minutes before a short fat guy materialized from the brush near the car. He was in full camouflage, his face streaked black and green, a GI-issue Kevlar helmet jammed on his head, a sawed-off 12-gauge shotgun in his hands. We climbed out and stood there uneasily as the rest of the crowd filtered silently out of the forest.

I didn't have a clue how well they could shoot but I'll say this for them—they had a good wardrobe consultant. About a dozen guys emerged from the trees looking like something out of *Apocalypse Now*. Heavy cammo makeup, knives and pistols on their belts, an assortment of weapons in their hands or slung over their shoulders.

They gathered in a loose semi-circle around us. If the thug who had cracked me over the head was among them there'd be no way to tell: their expressions were hidden not only behind camo paint but also behind a studied neutrality—or indifference. The sort of flat eyes you see in guys who don't care at all whether you live or die. None had rank insignia but one guy stepped forward in a formal way.

"Welcome, gentlemen," he said. "Mr. Bowen, how are you? And this is your friend Mr. Tripp?" He shook hands politely with each of us. The man was tall, probably six-two, six-three, with a large head that seemed even larger in the camouflage paint. He was all business. "For your reference, I'm Captain Lima. Your escorts today will be Lieutenants Bravo and Victor." With that two guys stepped forward, nodded, and then stepped back into rank. One of them carried a Herstal P-90, a lethal little weapon that along with waffles was one of the prides of Belgium: it could spit out 50 NATO rounds with one trigger squeeze and was accurate to a distance of two football fields. The last time I'd seen one of those was in the hands of a Serb soldier in Bosnia.

"A few preliminaries," said Captain Lima. "First, no real names here. While we have a constitutional right to do what we're doing, the government in its many forms continues to threaten us with arrest and prosecution. So we protect our identities. Clear?" Bowen and I looked at each other and nodded. "The second thing is I'm afraid we need to search you. Lieutenants." With that B and V approached.

Bowen put up his hands as though to stop them. "Jim, this is silly. You know I don't carry a gun."

"It's Lima," the man said sharply, "and it's not weapons I'm concerned with. The biggest threat in this country right now's the government-controlled news media. And they will do anything to sneak in those little cameras. Gentlemen." With that the lieutenants patted us down thoroughly. No cameras, but they confiscated my pocket knife.

"Excellent," said Lima when they'd finished. "Gentlemen, you'll join us? Lieutenants?"

With that Bravo and Victor barked out a series of commands and the squad moved off in a remarkably good approximation of a military unit on patrol: the short heavy man with the 12-gauge took point, the others following at intervals of five or ten yards. They placed us about midway back in the column with the captain. One of the lieutenants took the tail end. We walked slowly—and noiselessly—through the forest for maybe twenty minutes. At one point, the man in the lead gestured with a closed fist and the column abruptly halted. Lima moved forward for a hushed conference as they checked their maps. I had the feeling that it was a show for our benefit, but I didn't say anything—nobody said anything all the time we were on the trail.

We started up again and walked for another twenty minutes before we came upon a small clearing which had been made into a rough camp: a couple of logs lay around a campfire pit and they'd rigged up a tarp-covered shelter in the nearby trees for spare gear. Though I hadn't actually expected to see any, there was no sign of Hawkin's fertilizer. The lieutenants ordered out a perimeter guard and Lima sat down on a log and invited us to join him.

"So," he said, holding out his canteen, "welcome to the Pintler Volunteers, Montana Militia. Water?" We both took a drink.

"Out here a long time?" I asked

"Three-day recon," said Lima. "We arrived late last night and we'll close up camp tomorrow. The schedule gets people back for work on Monday."

Out here was a stretch of lonely mountain about thirty miles southwest of Pintler near the state line with Idaho, an area loosely referred to as the West Fork. It was known for good fishing, quite a few bears, and no people. Bowen and I had been up since before dawn getting here.

The squad had gathered around in a loose circle and broke out field rations—MREs, just like the regular army, Meals-Ready-to-Eat. Grunts called them Meals-Rejected-by-Everyone. Lima offered us one and Bowen accepted. I'd had them before: I passed.

"Three-day recon?" I said.

Lima nodded, opening a tinfoil packet and eyeing the contents suspiciously. "You ever in the service?"

I nodded, wondering silently to myself what Lima—Jim—did in real life. Maybe insurance, like Ed Woolsey.

"Then you probably know recon. We establish a base camp then do a grunt and shuffle through the woods for a couple of days. It hones their map skills, makes them alert to their environment. We work some ambush problems, night perimeters, things like that."

I'd expected less professionalism and told him that, complimenting him on the column we'd just walked.

Lima nodded. "There's a lot of misperceptions out in the world, Mister Tripp. One is that we're a bunch of amateurs playing soldier." Crooked grins showed from a few of the men gathered around us. "There's nothing playful about this, I'm afraid. We're out here to be as professional as we can be." Lieutenant Victor joined the group, resting his Herstal against his knee.

"P-90," I said. "Nice weapon. Last time I saw one of those was in Bosnia."

The lieutenant smiled and wiped his hand along the short barrel.

"The men are responsible for arming themselves," said Lima. "The constitution gives us the right to own and bear arms."

"Automatic arms?"

"Our interpretation of the law. They're a little more difficult to come by, but not impossible."

"But they're illegal."

"Only in some people's minds."

"I read in the press you have some fifty-caliber stuff?"

"I don't think I'd admit it if we did," smiled Lima,

chewing his MRE. "But we don't. There's no reason to. It would only invite the feds to swoop down on us and we'll get plenty of heavy stuff like that from the regular army when the day comes."

"The day?"

"The day the whole thing unravels." Lima stopped chewing and gave me an icy stare. This guy had to be more than a few sandwiches short of a picnic. "A lot of the regular army will come over to our side and bring their weapons along. You'll see."

"I didn't know the army was about to desert," I said, careful to keep a neutral smile on my face. Bowen sat there eating silently, watching the two of us.

Lima returned the smile, but it was without humor. "You're our invited guest, Mister Tripp, so we'll keep this cordial. And I'd like you to go away from this experience smarter than when you came. Fair?"

"Fair enough."

"So a couple of things you should know. We're a professional unit. We're all volunteers, we train hard, make a lot of sacrifices for this, because we believe in it." Nods from some of the grunts. "The press calls us paranoid and delusional. We think they're"—he seemed to search for a word—"misguided, or bought off. We're here because things are getting out of control." More nods from the others. Lima took a drink from his canteen and pushed his MRE aside. "I won't give you the full lecture: you don't have the time and I lecture too much as it is." Smiles from the assembled warriors. "The problem today is that the government's moving beyond the control of its own people. It's now almost exclusively owned by money—the money of the arms industry, trans-national companies, the money of wealthy foreign governments and foreign interests. It doesn't answer anymore to the people it's meant to serve. Now, one of our basic constitutional guarantees is the right to remove the government if it stops serving the people who put it in place. We all know that, right?'' He didn't wait for an answer. ''But how do we remove it? The ballot box won't do it. To win elections you have to have a national voice. But the media—controlled by the government—will never allow a national voice to the true patriots. So if not the ballot, the bullet.'' Nods from among the men and they looked at me for a response.

''Actually,'' I said, ''I don't disagree with a lot of what you're talking about. The problem is, I think you're utterly full of it if you think the bullet's the way to solve things.'' Bowen gave me a sideways glance and the soldiers seemed to tense up. Tough. I didn't come up here to have a love fest with a bunch of militia jerks. ''You start squeezing off rounds and setting off bombs, it's shoe salesmen and school kids who fall down dead, not a government. And certainly not a trained army. Those guys'll eat you for breakfast.''

Lima stood up abruptly and shouted out a command. The men around us jumped to their feet and hustled across to the far side of the clearing where they formed up in a single line. The captain glanced at us and then nodded to the lieutenant with the Herstal who turned to the unit and barked out something. The men fell to their stomachs and began belly-crawling through the brush, their weapons held slightly above their heads.

Bowen shot me an exaggerated wide-eyed glance and I gave it back with my eyes crossed.

The lieutenant dropped to his knees and let off with a long clawing spray of automatic fire just above the heads of the crawling soldiers. Captain Lima caught us with a quick look and a slight smile. The lieutenant reloaded his weapon and sprayed another burst just above the men.

"Live fire," said Lima, his voice almost purring. "Nothing better for training. Gives them a sense of what it's really all about." With a deliberate movement he pulled a grenade off his web belt, flipped out the safety pin and tossed it casually just a few feet away from us to the side of the crawling column. I dove across the log and knocked Bowen to the ground as the grenade erupted with a concessive explosion that seemed to swallow the air around us. Lima was staring down at us, smiling. "Flash-bang," he said. "It can't hurt you—there's no shrapnel. A practice grenade. You can get up." What a stupid, pointless stunt. I was angry enough to knock his teeth in—see how much he smiled after I yanked his head off his shoulders.

Bowen and I stood, dusting the pine needles from our clothes and I was about to say something truly nasty when Lima issued another command and the forest was swallowed in a roaring barrage of small arms fire. The militia had turned as a unit toward the other side of the clearing and was hammering the forest canopy with everything their weapons could offer.

I went back over and sat down on the log as the firing continued, working to bring my anger under control. I knew it wouldn't help. At length Lima gave his lieutenant a hand signal and the firing abruptly stopped. The men got to their feet safetying their weapons as a cloud of bitter blue smoke drifted slowly across the campsite.

Lima turned back to the two of us. "We can deliver an effective line of fire when the occasion arises," he said dryly. "What do you think?"

"I think you're nuts," I said.

"Thank you. Mister Bowen?"

"I try never to disagree with my friend," said Bowen.

Lima smiled like a man savoring a private joke. "When the time comes," he said, "we'll be ready. Lieutenants, work the men through the horseshoe. Now!" With that, Bravo and Victor snapped out a series of quick commands and the men formed up in a loose line and filed off into the forest. Lima turned back toward us. "Ambush practice. So Mister Bowen said you had some business about the dead rancher. Speak."

"Carson Woolsey," I said, working to keep my voice level. "He died during the winter. Somebody went to a fair amount of effort to make it look like an accident. It was murder."

"I heard he died," said Lima. "I didn't know it was murder."

"Some people have pointed their fingers at you."

"And my motive?"

"That's not quite as clear. A grudge maybe?"

"We don't kill people, Mister Tripp."

"You know him—knew him?"

"We knew him well. For a couple of years. Woolsey provided us space to train. He allowed us to conduct manoeuvres there for a couple of years."

"His ranch?"

Lima nodded. "High up, where the ranch runs into

the wilderness area. As long as we stay off government lands, the government generally tends to stay off our backs. He gave us the use of some of his space.''

''You say it in past tense?''

''He stopped it. One day he got word to us that we couldn't use the property anymore.''

''One day?''

''Four years ago,'' said Lima. ''Right about the time of the big muster.''

''Muster?''

''A rally, actually. A fifty-state rally of the militias over in Idaho. We trained hard for it. That was the summer Woolsey kicked us off.''

''Reason?''

''He didn't offer one. We'd used his mountains maybe a dozen times over a couple of years. Then I got word one day from him that it was no longer possible. That was it.''

''You ask him why?''

''Of course. I went out to see him. A safe training ground's a strategic resource for us. But he didn't have an answer. He just said it was no longer possible. So, of course, we never went back there.''

''And he never gave you a reason?''

''None.''

''Was Woolsey a member of your group?''

Lima arched his eyes slightly at the question. ''A patriot. Concerned, like us. But not a member.''

''But he let you use his property?''

''A patriot, nothing more.''

''I heard there'd been bad blood between you.''

Lima seemed amused by the comment. ''Not that I knew of. We had a business arrangement. It ended, simple as that.''

"Business arrangement?"

"We gave him money, he gave us space."

"You gave him money?"

Lima laughed out loud. "You think patriotism's free?"

"You paid to use his ranch?"

"Dearly."

"How much?"

"A couple of thousand."

"Each time?"

Lima nodded. "Each time."

"Where do you get that kind of money?"

The secret smile again. "Not all patriots are paupers."

"So you paid Woolsey to use the ranch?"

"Paid him well. Then one day he says the deal's off."

"You have any contact with him after that?"

"None."

I thought about the paranoid bartender and his strange, frightened visit to my motel room. "Some people get very nervous when I ask about you in Pintler. Any idea why that might be?"

Lima chuckled. "Ah, that would be Mister Wolf, wouldn't it." The chuckle again. "That's all right, Mister Tripp, I don't expect you to name your sources. Mister Wolf is a very strange man. He tried joining our group a few years ago but we wouldn't have him. Full-blown alcoholic, delusional, paranoid. Maybe a better description is he's just plain nuts. He's been trying to get even ever since. A street light goes out in Hamilton, he tells the police it's the militia."

"The man I had a chat with seemed mighty frightened."

Lima was still smiling. "He should be more concerned about his liver than us."

I looked around the camp. "I was up in the hills above Woolsey's ranch the other day and found a scrap of an old fertilizer bag. Hawkin's fertilizer. Ring a bell?"

Lima gave me an impassive look. "We're familiar with fertilizer, if that's what you're asking. It's part of the people's arsenal. But we haven't mixed any for years on Woolsey's place."

"Nothing last summer?"

"We weren't there last summer."

"What have you heard about his disappearance?"

Lima barked a short laugh. "I heard we killed him." He gave me a hard stare straight into the eyes. "We don't kill people, Mister Tripp. Not yet."

"A LOT OF FIRE POWER," said Bowen. We were back in his Jeep headed off the militia's mountain toward Pintler—both glad to be gone.

"What'd you think of them?" I asked.

"I think they're nuts," said Bowen.

"I thought they were your buds?"

He shot me an irritated glance from the corner of his eye.

We drove for a while in silence, the tires kicking up a stream of dust like a jet contrail behind us. We'd found no signs of Hawkin's fertilizer so that had been a dead end. Maybe Lima was lying to me about his relationship with Woolsey, and I couldn't prove it if he was. But I couldn't even begin to see a hint of why they'd bother with killing someone like Woolsey. No reason on the face of it. And it seemed to me that if this group was going to commit that kind of crime, take that kind of risk, it'd be on a target more politically significant than an obscure rancher.

The meeting, though, had provided a couple of new pieces of information that hadn't been in the puzzle before. Woolsey had been making money—good money—off the militia. A dozen training camps at a couple of thousand a shot is more than just pocket money. So there were some things about old Woolsey that weren't quite apparent. Maybe he wasn't just the simple old rancher everyone described. And Lima had said they got along fine with Woolsey until four years ago. From two widely separated sides now I had word of something happening in Woolsey's life about four years before: The realtor had told Pat that Woolsey had put the ranch on the market for a short time four years before. The militia had been told to stay away, four years before. What had been strong enough to make him give up that kind of money? And were they somehow connected?

In my previous life that kind of convergence—some people would call it coincidence—that kind of intersection of two separate paths could offer real possibilities. It used to come up so often I actually gave it a name—the Buried Bull Theory. Some ancient tribe tries to bury an enormous bull but it's so huge they can't get the horns all the way into the ground. A thousand years later another tribe comes along and is struck by the eerie coincidence of two identical horns sticking out of the ground. It's so unexplainable they build a religion around it. The mystery wouldn't be quite so great if they just shovelled a little dirt and found the connections. I had a set of horns now—and it was time to shovel a little dirt.

FOURTEEN

BACK IN PINTLER, Bowen went off to find Mike Woolsey to see what he knew about events on the ranch four years before and I headed toward the clinic. Hornick was in but seeing patients. She waved to me once from the hallway and gave me a nice smile but I had to wait another half hour before she came out and led me back to her office. Her black hair was messed and stiff and a puffiness under her eyes said sleep had been a rare commodity. "Sorry, but it's been one of those days around here." She gave me a pinched smile. "How are you?"

"Getting more sleep than you."

She tried smoothing back her hair. "We had the rodeo in town last night, and the cowboys broke everything in sight. I used so much plaster I'm beginning to feel like a sculptor. What news with you?"

I filled her in on the morning with the militia.

"They indoctrinate you?"

I smiled. "Made me a colonel and gave me a gun."

"Watch those boys. They're strange."

"Very strange," I said and sketched out for her how they'd trained on the Woolsey land but then been told they couldn't return. That it had happened four years ago.

Hornick nodded. "Four years ago, huh? I wonder..." She picked up the phone and dialed. "Jolene there?" she said into the receiver, looking at me but listening to the phone. "It's Pat. Tell her I called?" She put down the phone. "My friend the realtor. It looks like I need to do a little historical research."

Nathan found me in the cafe on my second cup of coffee, Ed Woolsey's ex working the counter and giving me a suspicious look from time to time. I pointed her out to him as he slid his large bulk into the booth and he reminded me that he'd known her for a long time. "Anything?" I asked.

"Not much, partner. I found the lad. Like he said before: he'd heard them back in the woods from time to time but he never knew his granddad had a deal with them."

Woolsey's ex approached the table and gave Bowen a shallow nod of recognition. Bowen ordered coffee and banana cream pie. I stopped the woman as she turned to go. "Quick question?"

She paused.

"Four years ago? Did something happen on the ranch? We heard it went up for sale briefly, for maybe a week or two?"

The woman looked at me blankly and I tried again. "A couple of people have told us that something happened on the ranch four years ago. Did you hear Carson put the ranch on the market?"

She was shaking her head. "News to me, I'm afraid. Sorry." She went back to waitressing.

"'Bout the same with me," said Bowen, offering a shallow shrug of his shoulders. "The boy didn't have much to offer. He said the sale thing was four years ago this summer. He didn't hear about it for a while and by the time he called to gripe, old Woolsey had pulled out of the deal.''

The ex-Mrs. Woolsey brought the pie and Bowen hit it like a coyote, managing somehow to talk between bites. ''He said he'd guessed the old man was tired of trying to keep the place up and had decided to sell. How's your nurse?''

''Doctor,'' I said and realized too late he was baiting me. ''Nothing much. Rodeo in town…''

''I heard.''

''…so she's busy patching bones. She tried calling the realtor but she's not around.''

''So maybe it's harmless. The old boy gets sick of running the place, decides to sell. Tells the militia to stay away. Seems to me I'd do the same thing. It'd be pretty tough to sell with a bunch of commandos running around in body paint.''

Back in the car, Bowen fished the portable phone out of the glove box where I'd stuck it. ''Have to keep this thing with you if you want it to work. Message on here.''

''Thing takes messages?''

He pushed a couple of buttons and listened. ''Your girlfriend the nurse called. Said to call her back. Here, I'll dial it for you, dipstick.'' He hit the buttons and handed me the phone. A couple of rings and then a voice: ''Pat Hornick.''

''Tripp,'' I said.

''Ben. I tried getting you.''

''What's up?''

''What do you know about mining?''

THE REALTOR'S OFFICE turned out to be one of the new pine-log buildings on the north side of town. Bowen and I pulled in just as Pat was getting out of her car.

"My friend Jolene called me back after you left," she said. "It turns out she's been doing some homework since the first time we talked. She called other realtors, went through the paperwork. She thinks she may have found something. She's not sure it's something, but it might be."

Jolene was old, short, energetic, and feisty. Grey hair cropped close to her scalp, a grey wool sweater over blue slacks. She led us to an office in the back with maps on the wall, stacks of books on shelves above a small desk, a computer with animated goldfish swimming across its screen.

"I started doing some homework after Pat called the first time," Jolene said. "I remembered the property coming on the market, and remembered being surprised when they took it off so fast." She picked up a black leather-bound office diary. "I dug this out and went back through my appointments for that period. A couple of local ranchers called about sub-dividing the property but I don't think they were too interested. Woolsey had it on the market for a million and a half. That's pretty stiff dosh for locals." She studied the book, running a calloused finger across the entries. "I had one call from a lawyer who said he represented a Hollywood movie star. He didn't say who. Redford, maybe. But I never got the chance to show the property. By the time he could fly in to see it, Woolsey had taken it off the market."

She closed the book with a snap and picked up a small notebook. "So I called some of my friends in the business. It's mostly the same for them: it's a long time ago but they remembered a couple of bites from

Hollywood, or L.A. at least, and a couple of locals with interest. But then a friend over at Montana Estates had something unusual. She said a company out of Nevada called her and actually flew some people in to look the place over. She went out with them. It was two fellows, nice enough she says, but obviously not ranchers. They had maps with them and spent a lot of time—most of two days—walking the property and making notes on their maps. She never heard from them again. A week or so later Woolsey took the property off the market."

Jolene closed the small book and looked up at us. "The weird thing was these guys kept stuffing rocks in their pockets."

"Rocks?"

Jolene nodded. "Rocks. My friend says they were picking up rocks all over the ranch. Not big ones, not boulders or anything like that, but small rocks that they stuffed in their pockets."

"What kind of rocks?"

Jolene gave me a quick off-center glance. "What do I know about rocks?"

"The name of the company?"

"She gave it to me," Jolene said looking down at her notes. "I've never heard of it before. Gordon Technology. Reno and Ontario. Gordon Technology. Think it means something?"

"And they were picking up rocks?"

"Rocks," said Jolene. "That's what my friend says. Picking up rocks and studying maps. My friend thinks they were miners."

ANOTHER THING about phones is they never work the first time—nobody's ever in when you try to call them or if they are in they don't have a clue what you're talking about. Bowen and I sat in the cab of his Jeep and called Gordon Technology in Reno to see what they might know about an old man and a ranch in Montana. Of course no one there had ever heard about Pintler or the Sula Basin and acted almost as though we'd slipped into another language. They gave us a number in Ontario and we got a little further there, or at least a little further up the company hierarchy— switched through two departments until we finally got someone who was helpful enough at first and then got cold feet and switched us to public relations who, of course, wasn't in and would call us back. I mention how much I hate telephones?

I got back to the ranch late, double-locked the door, and went down exhausted, dreaming guns and bad things. A nightmare woke me up at some point and I checked the door to make sure it was locked and spent a while sitting in the dark looking out the window. Then I had a tough time getting back to sleep.

The next morning came on tired and ragged and I didn't manage to get much accomplished. Bowen's phone went off mid-morning: Gordon Technology, Ontario, Canada returning my call and some uptight little bureaucrat with a high-pitched voice and an attitude who told me that company business was company business and certainly none of my business and have a nice day. I was beginning to wonder if all of middle age was going to be this nasty.

I tossed the phone on the bed, loaded up the fly rod, and drove up into the mountains to slay brook trout for the rest of the day. I got home late to find a piece of paper wedged in the door of my cabin: Roberta Feldy had been by with a bottle of wine and an empty evening. She'd left the wine on the table under the tree. Have a good day. I called her and, of course, she wasn't in. I drank the bottle and staggered off to bed.

It was a little after two when I came out of the wine with a sour stomach and banging head. Cold as charity in the cabin, and just about as black. A soft grunt from outside. The bear again. I padded up to the door, opened it a crack and yelled out, "Go away!"

A fist slammed into my gut like a piston. I stagger backward bent double and another blow smashes into the side of my head and the room spins and somehow I'm on my back and I sense a boot coming at me and I snake to the side and the kick grazes my hip and a man's guttural voice is taunting about how I couldn't stay away or something like that and I'm back on my feet and he's a squat heavy form in the darkness moving now to his left and I'm circling and trying to catch my breath. His fist moves through the darkness but I block it with my arm and counter hard with a right that glances somewhere off his face.

The form staggers backward and I wade in with a flurry of rights and lefts and he's grunting with the blows and I land a shot to the center of his face and it seems like he's collapsing. I ball my two hands into a single fist and swing hard into the side of his head. It rocks him back and he crashes against the doorjamb. I come in hard at his dark form, landing a series of shots into his gut and then he dodges out of my reach and I sense a fist coming at me and I duck low and it grazes me below the eye and I counter with another couple of shots that back him toward the door.

I straighten up for an instant and don't even see it coming as his boot takes me full in the crotch and it's like someone's ripping my intestines out with white-hot metal hooks. I slump to the floor, fighting to find my breath in the paralyzing pain. The guy is stumbling backward out of the cabin and it's almost like a dream sequence as I push myself up from the floor and lunge toward the door. I see him running through the darkness toward the trees, some sort of duffle or pack swinging from his arm. I start to run after him but my legs are like rubber and I trip and tumble into the dust. I manage to stand up again but he's gone.

Back in the cabin I poured myself a double shot of whiskey and took it in a single gulp. Somehow a part of me had been expecting him—that's why I was still alive. Ever since I'd found the torn-up meadow and picked up the tail on the way into Pintler, I knew that he'd come back. And I knew that when he came— whoever he was—it wouldn't be to just warn me. He'd come to kill me. The stakes now were as high as they get. The next time I'll drive the man into the ground.

FIFTEEN

THE PAIN in my crotch had backed down to a dull ache by the time I got to the university the next morning and found the man I needed to talk to. I took a seat in the back row as John Hunt was finishing up a lecture to an auditorium of probably four hundred sleepy freshmen.

I'd known Hunt for a couple of years—he'd helped me out with a case where a covetous university professor had killed a graduate student. Hunt had been a graduate student himself then but now had his doctorate and was teaching paleontology at the university in Missoula—as he put it, until real work came along. Real work for Hunt was chasing dinosaur bones in dusty trenches. The bell rang and he walked up, a dubious grin on his face. "So, the learned detective. What brings you to town?"

"The world's not a safe place," I said, shaking his hand. Hunt stood well over six and a half feet and had to duck to get through most doorways. I always felt physically small around him even though I'm a little more than six feet myself. He was a constant reminder that all things are relative.

Hunt was eyeing the scratches on my face. "Cut yourself shaving?"

"Midnight visitor."

"So this probably isn't completely a social call?"

"Buy you a cup of coffee?"

We found a table in the student cafeteria and I filled him in on the car wreck and the dead Carson Woolsey, the attack in the alley, the torn-up meadow, and my visit with the militia.

"And the scrapes on your face?" said Hunt, his eyes intent and his mouth serious. "I don't suppose I need a doctorate to figure out they're tied in to it?"

"Decent guess."

"So it's rough?"

"It's rough."

"And you need help?" he said.

"I need help," I admitted.

"Name it."

"Woolsey briefly had the ranch on the market four years ago but pulled it off after a couple of weeks. All really strange. Now we find out it looks like a mining company might have been interested. I'm not a miner."

"Neither am I," said Hunt dubiously. "I'm a bone hunter."

"I didn't know where else to look."

"The last time you asked me for advice, things got a little more exciting than I'm used to. Same sort of thing?"

"Maybe."

"But mining—geology—right?"

I nodded.

"Too far off my field," said Hunt. "Why don't we take a stroll. Somebody I think maybe you should meet."

With that, Hunt led me to a relatively new building tucked off to the side of the main university campus

and a lab lined with computers and rows of sophisti-
cated-looking machines. Almost every spare surface in
the room seemed covered by rocks and the floor was
gritty with dust. A woman with dark curly hair was
taking notes from one of the computers and turned as
we walked in.

"Hey Vic," said Hunt. "Brought an outsider
around for a visit. Doing anything sexy? Ben, Vicki
Brandon. Ben Tripp."

She smiled at the introduction and offered a handshake that was like the grip of a vise. "Afraid it's
nothing very sexy this morning. What's up?" Vicki
had intense blue eyes in an attractive rounded face—
mid-30s probably, a look about her that said tough and
smart. Her blue jeans were faded and her tee shirt
advertised beer.

"Ben needs some geology," said Hunt. "Figured
that new doctorate you nailed to the wall was just the
ticket."

Vicki flashed a smile that seemed to light up the
whole room. "We've got a lot of geology here. Any
particular type?"

"Cattle ranch type," I said and gave her a quick
outline of Woolsey's death and my conversations with
the various players. She arched her eyes and exchanged glances with Hunt when I mentioned how I
had found the scrap of paper from the fertilizer bag.

"What is it you're after?" she asked.

"A company called Gordon Technology sent some
people out to look at the place. We think they might
have been miners. I'd like to know what they might
have been after. I admit I don't even know if it's important, but it's about all I've got going."

"Gordon Technology?"

I nodded. "Four years ago. Two guys flew in and spent a couple of days on the ranch picking up rocks and making notes on maps."

"Sounds like miners," she said.

"That's what I thought, too."

"Let's go next door," she said and led us across a hall into a large room with shelves of books and manuals, a couple of serious-looking computers, and tray after tray of maps. Vicki sorted through several before she found what she was looking for and spread it out on a desk. It was like no map I'd ever seen before: I could make out the rough shape of the Sula Basin and the wilderness area around it and could identify the major roads, but the area was overlaid in broad swaths of reds, oranges, and greens.

"It's a geologic map of the area," said the woman. "Shows us what's under the ground. Where exactly are you talking about here?"

I oriented us on the map by tracing the main highway out of Pintler and then following the smaller country road up to the Woolsey ranch. The area showed up as a broad band of red touched here and there with a narrower line of bright green.

Hunt and I hovered over her as Vicki ran her finger down a color chart in the margin. "Intrusive. Some pyroclastics here and there. But it's mostly intrusive."

I gave her a questioning look.

"A type of rock," he said. "It's mostly intrusives in the area. But there's a good band of pyroclastics along here."

"Which means?"

"Absolutely nothing at this point. It's a pretty common type of rock. Let me try another map," she said, digging around in some more trays and pulling out another chart. This one had less color and was banded in contour lines and dotted thickly with numbers. "An old government map," said Vicki. "It shows elevation and primary structures."

We managed to locate the black dot that represented the Woolsey ranch. An inch away from that dot was a tiny stylized picture of a crossed pick and shovel. There was another a half inch further on.

"Ever hear of mining up there?" asked Vicki.

"There's some old mining roads."

Vicki was nodding. "The little picks and shovels are mines. There's no way to tell from this what they were mining, but there's been some activity up there. I bet it's pretty old, though. This map is ancient." She studied it some more and then slipped it back into the tray. "So, we've got some pretty good metamorphics, a touch of pyroclastics, and some old mines. Interesting."

"Interesting?"

"Why don't you guys give me a few minutes," she said, sitting down at one of the computers and firing it up. "I'll catch you outside."

Hunt and I perched on the front steps and watched girls for nearly half an hour before Vicki emerged, stretching and yawning, through the front doors. We made a place for her between us.

"So?" said Hunt.

"I ran the data bases," Vicki answered, "but it was a dry hole. Not a thing about mining or mineralization on your friend's ranch. I searched all the data on that part of Montana. It doesn't mention the Sula Basin at all."

"Nothing, huh?"

"Not a thing. I also ran a search on Gordon Technology. It's a huge company, like billions and billions of dollars huge, but it's mostly some sort of holding company. No mining that I could find. Sorry.''

"So we're stuck?" I said, and my voice must have hit a sour note because Vicki shot me a sideways glance.

"Stuck?" she said in an exaggerated way. "Me, stuck?"

Hunt was smiling beside her, like they were sharing some secret joke.

"What am I missing?"

"You don't know Vicki Brandon," said Hunt. "We call her the bulldog."

"Me, a bulldog?" said Vicki in a feigned tone of injury.

"Lady bulldog."

"That's better."

Hunt grinned. "Lady bulldog like in when she gets something in her teeth, she won't let it go 'til it's thoroughly chewed."

Vicki made a low growl and then flashed the megawatt smile again. "We haven't even banged any rocks yet."

"I just love to bang rocks," said Hunt dryly.

"And I love field trips," said Vicki. "We've gotta have Cheetos. Can't bang rocks without Cheetos."

SIXTEEN

THE THREE OF US met early the next morning, loaded rock hammers and maps in my pickup, made a stop for junk food, and were at the Woolsey ranch by ten. It was a cloudless day this time and we could clearly make out the track up across the face of the hill and the darker spot at the spring where I'd discovered the fresh tire tracks. I dropped the pickup into low and we crawled across the pasture tracks.

"That outcrop up there?" said Vicki, gesturing toward the top of the first hill. "The light-colored rock?"

I nodded.

"Probably some sort of tuff," she said.

"Tuff?"

"Volcanic. Not really lava. It's more like the heavy flows you get of ash and melted rock." Vicki spread a map across Hunt's lap and hers—it was crowded in my truck—and studied the colors. "This thing shows some pyroclastics—some volcanics—in the area generally. But it's not specific enough to show each bedding."

"Important?" I asked.

"Hard to know," said Vicki. "It depends if there's anything in the rock that's valuable."

We reached the top of the hill which had been

shrouded in fog on my last trip up. This time we could see for miles in all directions and make out the path of the dirt road as it snaked up and through a series of gentle rises. I spotted the place where it disappeared into the trees: the meadow was just beyond.

Hunt was eating Cheetos and Vicki was providing a running commentary on the landscape. "Coming up on the flanks of a pretty good syncline here. See those pinkish rocks over there? Pretty good pyroclastics, I suspect. But there's some granite mixed in here too so I'd bet we're sort of on the edge of a contact zone."

"Important?"

"Maybe. It means we're along the border where an old volcanic region edged up against a bed of meta-morphics."

"And that means what?"

"I suppose you could picture it like this," she said. "A long time ago this was probably a river valley, something like that. The sediment—mud and rocks— gets laid down over millions and millions of years and builds up until it's miles deep. The weight creates heat and pressure that changes the sediments into a kind of rock, a metamorphic rock—granite, something like that. Then along comes Mister Volcano and squeezes up through the middle. We're right on the edge of where that volcano came up through the granite. That's what the map shows anyway."

We followed the road along the wall of fir tree I'd remembered from the time before and came, suddenly, on the small meadow. But it wasn't the same. I pulled the pickup to a stop and surveyed the scene in aston-ishment: since my trip up here just a week before, someone had been in here working. Fresh dozer tracks showed as new scars in the red soil. The area that had been scraped down to hard rock a week ago now had a new smooth covering of dirt over it. The pit where I'd found the yellow scrap of the fertilizer bag had been completely filled in, a layer of brown soil graded over the top. The area that had been griddled off with the small piles of rocks had been flattened, wiped clean. I killed the engine and sat there for a moment in silence.

"Problems?" said Vicki, eyeing the scene.

"Gone," I said. "Everything's been changed." I got down from the truck and wandered across the fresh topsoil.

Hunt came up beside me. "You were here when?"

"A week ago."

He whistled softly. "Quick work."

"Yup." Ambivalent feelings. Losing a clue was losing time, losing ground. But losing the clue was a clue in itself. Someone had gone to a lot of work to cover the area. Regular ranching activities? Hard to see how. If Woolsey was the one who scraped the trench out in the first place—or blasted it out—it certainly wasn't Woolsey who filled it in sometime in the last week. And Westlands had said they weren't even up in the mountains. So, if no Woolsey, no Westlands, who? And, just as important, why? Why dig out a hole in a mountain only to come back a year later and fill it in?

"What was here before?" asked Vicki.

I walked across the new flat surface. "Under here," I said, "they'd scraped away the topsoil down about two feet or so, down to a sort of reddish or rust-colored rock."

Vicki bent down and picked up a small stone. "Like this?"

"Like that," I said. She slipped the rock into her pocket. "But it was a big area," I said, "probably about the size of a football field. Then over there"—I gestured with my arm—"over there they'd dug a trench maybe twenty feet wide, five or ten feet deep." I walked to the spot where I guessed it had been. "I couldn't figure that one out."

Vicki had her hammer out and was pounding on another rock. "Tuff," she said. "Pyroclastic flow. Nice little fellow. He looks kind of spongy, see." She pulled out a small magnifying glass and studied it closely. "It looks pinkish or rust-colored from a distance. But that's actually these little crystals in it, see?"

"What's that?" I asked, pointing at the lens in her hand.

"The crystals?"

"No, the magnifying glass? It's a jeweler's loupe, isn't it?"

"Yeah," said Vicki, giving me a blank look.

"Geologists use those?"

"All the time. Why?"

"I found one in Woolsey's nightstand." My mind ranged back on that day. I'd found the loupe in his nightstand—and I'd come across a book on gems and minerals in his half-packed living room. Coincidence? Or buried horns? "What about the crystals?"

Vicki put the loupe back up to her eye and studied the rock. "Well, it's hard to say. Any time you get pyroclastics like this you can get some pretty good mineralization. There could be anything in this stuff, or nothing at all."

"Like...?"

"Well, there could be antimony, arsenic, thallium, things like that."

"Which means...?"

"Not much in itself. But you get an arsenic halo, that's what they call it, an arsenic halo, then you start to get interested."

"Get interested...?"

Vicki nodded. "Start seeing arsenic or thallium, antimony, you perk up quick. Gold hangs out in the same general neighborhood."

"You said gold?"

"Gold. As in AU." Her face was serious.

"There's gold in that rock?"

"Impossible to tell from looking at it. And no one would go running to the bank yet on this piece of stuff. Usually it's some other mineralization—zinc, silver, something like that. You'd have to analyze it, find out what's in there. It's a long process."

Hunt had loaded his pockets with rocks and was carrying another about the size of a melon to the pickup. He came back up to us dusting his hands. "I know Vicki," he said. "She likes lots of rocks."

"There was also a grid-like thing," I said. "Little piles or rock on the corners and along the sides."

Vicki shot me a questioning glance. "How big?"

"About the size of a football field."

Vicki was nodding her head. "Why don't we see where this road goes," she said. "I've got a pretty good hunch there's something else up here we might want to take a look at."

This time I was the one who formed the question in my eyes.

"Trust me," she said, turning on her laser smile.

We got back in the truck and drove slowly up the

narrow dirt path. Beyond the meadow the road entered a thick band of fir trees and the daylight dimmed in the undergrowth. Emerging back into the sunshine, we crept along a narrow shoulder where the road had been cut back into the rock.

"Jeez, slow down," said Hunt, rolling down his window and peering out at the rock. "Looks a lot like some pretty good bedded turretella."

"Not in this stuff," said Vicki.

"Betcha."

"You're on," she said as they clambered out. I pulled the pickup to a stop as the two banged and pried at the rock. They were still arguing when they climbed back in.

"Something important?" I asked.

"Nothing," said Vicki. "Hunt thought he saw Tyrannosaurus Rex in there."

"It looked like limestone," said the tall man defensively.

"Hunt sees T-Rex in everything."

We'd gone another two miles or so when Vicki suddenly told me to pull over. We all climbed out and she led us up a narrow trail that had been cut into the bank above the road. At the top of the trail, the firs and brush had been cleared away in an area at least a hundred yards long, the same width. More bulldozer tracks in the torn-up earth and a neat pattern of six piles of gravel, each about five feet high, in a rough rectangle across the clearing.

Vicki bent down next to one and put her face almost to the dirt, digging into the gravel with her hands. After a moment she stood up and slapped the dirt from her knees.

"What?" I said. My voice had an edge to it.

"I think we've got something," she said.

"What?"

"We follow this road, we should find another place just like this. I'd bet some pretty serious cash on it."

"Another place like this? What is this place?"

The laser smile was gone. "We've got some big-time prospectors working here, that's what."

"Prospectors?"

"That meadow back there, the first one?" said Vicki. "Obviously we can't see it now, it's been covered up. But from your description, it sounded to me like we had some exploration going on. Then you mentioned the area that was gridded out. That's a dead giveaway. It's exploration, it's how we do it. But the trick here is you never explore just in one place. It doesn't tell you anything. You've got to spread it out, see how big the deposit is. So we come along this road here, and sure enough, here's another one."

Vicki gestured toward the small piles of gravel. "Each of those is a drill hole. Somebody's been up here with a drill rig punching holes in the ground to see what's down there." She walked from one pile to the next. "It's the regularity that gives it away. They've mapped out a grid pattern here and dropped exploratory holes to see what's under here. They did a full survey, by the looks of it."

"Who's 'they'?"

"Prospectors, obviously."

"Prospecting for what?" I pressed.

"We can't know," answered Vicki. "It could be anything from zinc to silver to gold. Or it could be nothing at all but I'd be surprised by that, with all the work somebody's putting into it." Vicki glanced up toward the mountains beyond us. "I figure we go on up that road another mile or two, we'll hit another patch just like this. Maybe more after that.''

Vicki loaded herself down with another collection of rocks and made me and Hunt carry more. We dropped them into the bed of the pickup and climbed in.

''Your scrap of paper from the fertilizer sack?'' said Vicki.

I nodded.

''I bet they made themselves a batch of explosives to loosen the rock. Dollars to donuts.''

After another mile or so the road emerged from the trees onto the shoulder of a fairly steep bare hillside and we edged along it until we came to a barbed wire gate. I pulled to a stop and looked out toward the south: in the valley eight or ten miles away I could clearly make out the silver roof of Woolsey's barn. From this distance, the Summey ranch looked right next door to it. I guessed the fence line we were at had to be the dividing line between the two ranches. I pointed the ranch out to Hunt and Vicki and told them about the strange meeting with Joe Summey and his paintings of the mountains.

The road came off the face of the hill after a quarter of a mile or so and into another high saddle, or small valley.

''Yup,'' said Vicki in a low voice as I pulled to a stop. Another torn-up patch of land. Six piles of gravel in a neat geometric pattern.

''This is a big sucker,'' said Hunt, his eyes shining. ''We must be four, five miles from the first site. Big sucker.''

''Huge,'' said Vicki.

''Same kind of rock?'' I asked.

Vicki was nodding. "Look at that the outcropping. Same rock."

"But a different ranch," I said softly.

As the two of them collected more rocks, I sat there chewing on what we'd discovered. Active mining exploration on both the Woolsey and Summey ranches—and for all intents and purposes a secret from the outside world. The question is whether they'd found anything—and how that tied in to an old man dying in a blizzard.

Hunt dropped an armload of stone into the back of the truck and he and Vicki climbed into the cab.

"Any guesses?" I asked. "I mean, from what you've seen?"

"Hard to say," said Vicki. "We've sure found where other people have been looking."

"You think they found something up here?" I asked, starting up the truck and heading back the way we had come.

Vicki seemed to be lost in concentration and took her time answering. "I bet they probably did. The way you do these things is really a three-step process. And you don't get to this step unless there's something there."

"Three steps?"

She nodded. "The first thing you do is kind of an initial survey. You study the maps, pick up rocks, do some stream sampling to see if anything's out there. You get all that stuff analyzed and if there's some hints, you take it to the second step."

I thought about the realtor Jolene and how the men from Gordon Technology had spent two days on the property, looking at rocks and checking their maps. It fit with Vicki's description. "The second step?"

"Really just a more complete survey than the first. More samples, more maps, things like that. If you took five samples the first time, you'd take maybe fifty the next time. Again, you put them in for analysis."

"Which is…?"

"Which is sort of a hi-tech test to see what's there," said Vicki. "It'll give you a rough idea of what you're dealing with."

"You said three steps?"

Hunt had gotten back into the Cheetos.

"The third step's expensive," said Vicki. "You've got to be pretty excited about something to do that. That's the drilling. Heavy equipment, a drill rig, and then an expensive full-spectrum analysis of what you've brought up. That costs tons—maybe like a couple of hundred thousand. It's not something you do unless you're pretty convinced it's going to pay off."

"And that third step's what we found today?"

"I'd say that's what we found today. I mean, I know it is."

"So somebody's pretty serious about this?"

"Extremely," said Vicki.

We drove in silence for a while.

"A couple of things about this seem off-center," I said after a while, more to myself than to the two next to me. "I mean no one has talked about any exploration up here." We were driving past the rough trail to the second exploration site and stared at it as we passed. "The other odd thing is it's not just on the Woolsey ranch but on the ranch next door, on the Summey ranch. I've talked to Summey. He didn't mention it."

"Somebody would have to know," said Vicki. "I mean you could camouflage the early stages, pretend to be a hunter or something like that and come up here and do a survey. But you start moving in bulldozers and drill rigs, that's pretty visible activity.''

''But we don't know what they're looking for,'' I said.

''Yet,'' said Vicki. ''We don't know yet, but we will.''

SEVENTEEN

I TOOK THE CELLPHONE with me that evening and waited for Hunt's call on Bowen's back porch. I was jumpy and it showed: I'd left Hunt to work the computer and Vicki Brandon to test the rocks. What they found would tell me where I was headed.

Bowen had some new gadget guaranteed to give knife blades a razor edge and was fiddling with it on the table. It had a couple of parallel bars on it and an elaborate clamping device designed to bring the blade down on the sharpening stone at some precise angle. I watched him as he set it up, decided it was wrong, and take it apart. Then he set it up again. The fiddling was about to drive me nuts so I tried reading the newspaper but didn't have the patience for that either. I slapped the paper down and stared at the phone.

"Won't help," said Bowen without looking up from his thing.

"I know that."

"You need a vacation."

"I need a vacation?"

"Or a hobby."

"What brought that on?"

"You just do." Bowen was sliding the knife against the stone. The sound had my teeth on edge.

"You think Hunt maybe lost the number?"

"I think you need a vacation more than a hobby. Go somewhere and lie on the sand. Or you need a date. What happened to that Robert Fielding woman?"

"Roberta Feldy. She's around." A little too much defensiveness in my voice: I didn't mention the part about her leaving the wine and me drinking it alone. "Had a black bear around the house couple of nights ago."

Bowen didn't even bother to look up. "Garbage cans?"

"Tulips." I didn't say anything about me chasing it around naked with a filleting knife.

"They like tulips?"

I just grunted.

"How's the nurse?" he asked, still intent on the device.

"Doctor."

"How's the doctor?"

"Haven't talked to her in a day or so."

"Should, you know. Quite a woman."

"Did you know she's Mormon?"

"I like Mormons."

"And Mexican," I added.

"I know they like bulbs," said Bowen.

"What?"

Bowen glanced up. "Bears. Saw one once in a patch of wild onions. Can you imagine what his breath must have been like?" He chuckled at the thought. "Tulips, huh?" Bowen tried the knife out on the newspaper. It cut a clean line, but nothing miraculous.

"How much'd you pay for that thing?"

"Guy gave it to me free. Wants me to sell it in the store."

The cellphone rang and I pushed the button but there was no one on the line.

"You hung it up, dipstick," said Bowen mildly. "Next time push the button with the little phone on it. See it?"

The phone rang again and this time I hit the right button. "Tripp here."

Hunt's voice on the other end. "You hung up on me."

"Sorry."

"I found some stuff in the computer."

"And...?"

"And, I traced the ownership. Both Summey and Woolsey hold the mineral rights up there—it's been in both families forever. The Summey claim goes back to 1895. The claim on the Woolsey place was filed in 1899."

"And that means what?" More impatience in my voice than I wanted but I couldn't help it.

Hunt's voice was just as tight: "No changes since then except for a couple of inheritances, but the claims have stayed in the families."

"Anything in there to show who might be doing the exploration?"

"Nothing."

"Is that normal?"

"I can't answer that, Ben. I just don't know."

"How's it going with the rocks?"

"Vicki's still at it," said Hunt, "but I think she's almost there. Should have something soon."

I put the phone down, staring distractedly at Bowen's gadget.

"News?" asked Bowen.

"Joe Summey and Carson Woolsey own the mountain."

"And exploration going on?"

"Looks that way."

"And somebody trying to cover it up?"

I nodded.

"And an old man dead?"

"Yup."

"And you're headed back to Pintler?"

"Nope. To a geology lab."

"Need a knife sharpener?"

I left Bowen with his new gadget and drove through nighttime Missoula to the geology lab. Hunt was sitting on a stool playing with a Bunsen burner and a blow pipe. Vicki turned as I walked in.

"Interesting samples," she said matter-of-factly. "I'm just finishing the last run." She wrote some notes on a pad. "I haven't had much time on this so it's extremely preliminary. I mean, I can't guarantee you that the science is all that good."

"Not a problem."

"Then let me show you what we've got," said Vicki. "First, I did a little more research on the area, especially the two old mines we found on the map." She opened a folder and spread a map out on the lab table. "Those symbols on the Woolsey ranch were, in fact, gold mines and were worked on and off from the 1890s up until about 1930. They must have been on a pretty good vein to stay active that long. But by the '30s it was exhausted and they were out of there."

"So the gold is gone?"

"Not in the way you think," said Vicki, her face serious. "It's a matter of economics and technology. In the old days, they didn't have the technology to move a lot of ore cheaply so they only hit the high-grade veins. An ounce of gold from a ton of rock was a pretty good payday. As they started getting less gold from each ton, the profit margin began to slip and they'd finally reach a point where there wasn't enough gold to pay for what it cost to mine it, so they closed down.''

''And that's what happened on Woolsey's place?''

''I suspect so,'' said Vicki. ''It's happened all around the world for centuries.''

''So no gold?''

''Not quite,'' she said, handing me a computer printout. Stacked down the left margin was a list of more than 30 elements, from aluminum and antimony to vanadium and zinc. Right in the middle, below gallium and above iron, sat gold. She'd marked it with a yellow highlighter. Next to it across the sheet were a series of numbers and percentages. I looked up at her.

''The lab report on the rocks wc hauled back,'' she said. ''Interesting stuff.''

Hunt spoke up. ''How interesting?''

Vicki gave him a shallow, edgy smile. ''Extremely.''

''Okay,'' I said, ''what's going on?''

The two exchanged a quick glance.

''You've stumbled on some pretty good mineralization,'' said Vicki.

My look must have been uncomprehending.

''Ever hear of the Carlin Mine in Nevada?'' she asked.

I shook my head.

''A big mine,'' she said. ''Two thousand miners moving two hundred million tons of ore a year. Any idea how much gold they're pulling out?''

I shook my head again.

"A million ounces."

"Sounds like a lot," I offered lamely.

"I'll translate that for you," she said. "A million ounces at current prices would be, oh, let's see, carry the one and subtract the two"—she flashed a tight grin—"right in the neighborhood of three hundred million dollars. A year. One mine. Three hundred million dollars worth of gold. Figure a profit margin of fifty percent, the owners are walking away with a hundred fifty million dollars a year."

"And that has what to do with us?" I asked, suspecting I already knew the answer and feeling my stomach tighten.

"It's the same kind of deposit," said Vicki. "It's on the sheet in front of you."

I glanced at the paper and then looked up again.

"See the line where it says 'gold'?" She leaned over my shoulder and pointed to it. "'Gold' right there. Now scan across. See what it says? Point zero three. That's how much gold's in each ton of rock up there."

"Is that a lot?"

"Not a lot a hundred years ago," said Vicki, "not even worth mining. Today, it's a lot. It's massive."

"I don't get it."

"Brand new technology," she said. "Brand new wealth."

"New technology?"

She nodded. "Cutting-edge."

"Like what kind of technology?"

"Remember I talked about mining the old high-grade veins?" said Vicki. "You probably wouldn't know it, but things have changed substantially, just in the last ten years. The old-timers started losing money when the concentrations of gold fell below about a tenth of an ounce in every ton. It's a whole new game today with the new technologies and the economies of scale you can bring to a big operation. You can make money today, lots of money, from concentrations of gold so small you can't see it without a microscope."

"No-see-ums," said Hunt, nodding his head.

"No-see-ums?" I said

"No-see-ums," Vicki parroted. "The actual scientific name is bulk tonnage disseminated deposits. It's also called sediment-hosted gold. You literally can't see the gold. The concentrations are up to a hundred times smaller than the old high-grade mines used to work. Microscopic. But it's still gold. And it's still worth a fortune."

"I've never heard of it," I said.

"Not surprising," answered Vicki. "It's really new-wave stuff—all the rage, and it's revolutionizing the industry. Big companies are going back into places abandoned for centuries and starting up gold mines. It's the hot new trend."

"How hot?"

"Probably the hottest thing in the industry today."

"And the rocks we brought back?"

"On the paper in front of you," said Vicki. "Rhyolitic tuffs. The main ore mineral is electrum and we pulled up trace amounts of arsenic-rich pyrite, pyrrhotite with silver sulfosalts like tetrahedrite, pyrargyrite, and gold-silver telluride."

"In English?"

Vicki grinned. "The key word there is gold-silver telluride. Scientific for gold. In trace amounts every bit as good as the Carlin Mine in Nevada. This one's a big mother. Could be bigger than Carlin.''

"Bigger than Carlin?" I said it almost reflexively, my mind spinning across the empty hills above the two ranches.

"Even if it's just half as big," said Vicki, "that's still a hundred fifty million dollars worth of gold a year. Carlin's been going at that rate for thirty years and they think there's enough gold under there to go for another seventy. Let's see, that would be—carry the one, subtract the two—oh, well, maybe, gee…ten billion dollars worth of gold, plus or minus the few-odd million.''

"Ten billion?"

"Ten billion," said Vicki. "Dollars."

"Wait a minute," I said. "I mean if that mountain's worth ten billion, someone would have figured that out by now."

"Wrong," said the woman. "I can't tell you how new this technology is. It's just getting started. Look at it this way. Figure there are maybe a million abandoned gold mines scattered around the world today—mines where the vein played out and it was worthless to keep going. Probably a million, maybe more. Know how many have been re-opened to sediment-hosted mining?"

I shook my head dumbly.

"Fewer than a dozen."

"And this could be one of them?"

"I'd stake my degree on it."

"Ten billion dollars worth of gold?"

"I'd stake my degree on that, too."

Ten billion dollars worth of gold. My mind washed across the meadow above the Woolsey ranch. A high desolate spot of nothing in a nowhere part of the world and under it a glittering dome of gold as big as a city. And just down the road an old man dead in a ditch. I now knew the motive. Now I had to find out who. And there was at least one man still alive who had to have an answer.

EIGHTEEN

THE STREAMS WERE STILL out of their banks, the cattle were still working the willow flats as I turned up the road to Sula Basin the next afternoon to talk to a man about a mountain of gold. I dodged a couple of puddles that had pooled across the blacktop and made the turn into the lane toward Joe Summey's ranch. A wooden gate I hadn't seen the last time was locked and I had to walk the last quarter mile. The house seemed lifeless and my knock on the door sounded hollow within. With suspicions growing that I wouldn't like what I'd find, I tried the knob but it was locked. I moved along the windows but the curtains hid the view.

Back at the front door, I pulled out my pocket knife and tried springing the lock but it wouldn't give. Frustrated, I gave the door a good solid kick and it sprang open with a loud bang. But I needn't have worried about the noise—there was no one there to hear it. The living room was empty. No furniture, no sign of life. The small table by the window where Summey and I had sat and talked about the colors of winter was gone. Gone too was the easel with Summey's outline of the mountains and the patch of sky blue. A few paint stains on the wooden floor was all that remained.

I checked through the rest of the house, but it was

equally abandoned. The kitchen had been packed up and moved out. Even the refrigerator was gone. I let myself out the back door and gazed up at the mountain beyond. Two men owned that mountain. One was dead. And now the other was gone.

BACK IN PINTLER I found Mike Woolsey at work in the grocery store and led him out to a bench on the sidewalk.

"I've been doing some checking," I said, "and a couple of things have come up. You hear anything about Joe Summey?"

Mike gave me a puzzled look. "Joe Summey?"

I nodded. "I was up at his place just now and he's gone."

"How gone?"

"Gone gone. Gone like in he's split. The house is locked up, empty, everything moved out. Heard anything about it?"

Mike was shaking his head. "Nothing. Boy, that's strange. He's lived up there forever. Any idea where he went?"

"You hadn't heard he was moving?"

Mike shook his head again.

"Any idea where he might go?"

"Sorry but no."

"You ever hear he had money problems?"

"Money problems?"

"Like he was broke or anything like that?"

Mike was still shaking his head. "Grandpa told me Summey got in way over his head back in the '80s, back when all the farmers were mortgaging themselves to the eyeballs. That the sort of thing you're talking about?"

"Could be," I said. "Any idea how deep he was in?"

"Sorry, but not really. Grandpa said the man had made some bad decisions. But we never really talked about it."

"Ever hear anything else about it?"

"Nothing really. I mean I remember they had an auction on his place when I was just a little kid. But I don't know if that was connected. Why the question?"

"Did anybody ever say anything about mining on your grandpa's ranch?"

The boy's eyes widened. "Mining?"

I nodded.

"Nothing like mining. Nothing. There's a couple of old mines up there but they've been out of business forever. What about mining?"

"Did your granddad know about them?"

"No. Well…I guess maybe yes is the answer. I mean he knew they were up there. But he didn't know about mining, anything like that."

My mind flashed back to the jeweler's loupe I'd found—and the book on gems and mineralogy. "You're sure he didn't know about mining?"

"Positive. I mean, that wasn't something he cared about. Why the questions?"

"I'm not quite sure," I admitted. "It looks like there's been some pretty active mining exploration back on your granddad's property—and on Summey's place as well. They may have found something."

"Found what?"

"Gold."

"Gold?" His eyes were wide.

I nodded.

The boy looked at me dubiously. "That's not something I've heard anything about. You're sure?"

"I'm sure."

"How much gold?"

"Let's just say a lot of it."

"And now Summey's gone," said Mike. "We've got to take this to the sheriff."

"I don't think so. More than one lawman's been bought with gold. You've got to keep it quiet, at least until I can unravel some more of this."

Mike's cheeks colored further. "And I was right: Somebody did kill grandpa?"

I nodded. "I think you were right, son. But keep your mouth shut and your head down. Let me find out who."

Mike gave me a grim look.

I left Mike outside the grocery store and drove the couple of blocks to his father's insurance office. I could see Ed through the window talking with someone so I parked down the street and waited. After maybe ten minutes Ed Woolsey walked the man to the door and waved him off down the street. He was back at his desk when I rang the bell and pushed into the small office.

Ed looked up with an eager expression but lost it fast when he saw me standing there. "Thought I told you to get lost?" he snarled, standing up and leaning his bum leg against the desk.

I smiled as pleasantly as I could but I guess it wasn't that pleasant. "Unfinished business."

"Not with me, buster. Take a hike." His lower lip was trembling in anger, and I marvelled at how quickly the fury had come over him.

"Easy Ed," I said, putting my hands out in front of me. "Just a few questions."

"Not with me."

"Like when did you make the deal with the mining company?"

The question seemed to stop him in his tracks, but not quite the way I'd wanted. I figured I'd throw the question, get an instant denial behind a shifty glance and have my man. Instead, he seemed genuinely confused about what I'd said. No shifty eyes, no criminal flinch of the shoulders, just a deep confusion across his face. "Mining company?"

"Mining company," I said, firmly.

"What mining company?"

"The mining company you and your dad did a deal with?"

"You're out of your mind. What mining company?"

I felt the moral high ground shifting slightly beneath my feet. "The one that's been up there on the ranch drilling for samples for the last year. That mining company."

"Are you a dope fiend?" said Woolsey, incredulously. "There's nothing like that up there. What are you smoking?"

I held my ground. "There's been a mining company up there at least since last summer taking drill samples. Just up the hill from the old gold mines."

Woolsey actually burst out laughing. "There's no gold up there. That all gone, has been for a lifetime. You're getting some bad information."

I pushed on, a hard edge to my voice. "Fact is there's something pretty valuable up there that people are hunting. Don't try to tell me you don't know about it.''

"I won't try to tell you anything, Mister Big Man Investigator from Missoula,'' snarled Woolsey. ''But the fact is I never went near that place more than I had to. There could be a Wal-Mart and a parking lot for all I know up there. News to me.''

"Seems to me reason enough to kill an old man.''

Woolsey barked out a nasty laugh. ''First you accuse me of killing the old boy to inherit. Now you're saying I killed him for a mine which doesn't have any gold in it. You're either dumb or crazy. The old man died in a car wreck.'' Woolsey came around from behind the desk. ''Now get out. For the last time.''

I started backing up toward the door. ''Somebody's working gold up there.''

"I'll see that for myself,'' Woolsey hissed, ''and I'll take care of it myself. Now you get out of my life and don't come back.''

I walked slowly across the street, climbed in my pickup, and sat there for a while. I could see Woolsey glaring at me through the window but I can't say it mattered much: I didn't expect I'd win a popularity contest with the man. And I have to admit that I liked him as a suspect. It fit, in a sick sort of way: a little man so convulsed by the promise of extraordinary wealth that he'd kill his father to get it. The problem was I couldn't reconcile the way he acted with the way I thought he should be acting, and I didn't have even an ounce of evidence connecting him with the murder.

With Ed Woolsey hovering both literally and figuratively in the shadows, my mind kept circling back to Joe Summey. Undeniable that he owned half the mountain. Undeniable that they'd been prospecting on his land. And undeniable that now he was gone.

But gone where? I ran down the possibilities. He'd mentioned Sante Fe. I'd have to check that. But if he'd actually decided to hide out, it could be tough to find him.

On an impulse that was more hope than hunch, I dug the cellphone out of the glove box and got a number for Pat's realtor friend, the one who had given us the first clue about mining on the Woolsey place. If Summey was truly gone, maybe the realtor had heard something about it. A machine at the office said they were closed and I left a message. I tried Pat at the clinic but they said she'd gone home early: they could page her if it was an emergency. It wasn't.

Dusk had begun to settle as I turned for the highway home. It felt like I was leaving a lot left undone, but for the moment anyway I'd run out of options in Pintler. Maybe a new day would bring new ideas. And then the truck started ringing again. It was the second time it had happened, but it still sent a small wave of panic through me before I realized it was the cellphone and managed to get it up to my ear.

"Is this the Tango King?" It was Pat's voice.

I grinned to myself in the dim light of the pickup cab. "You got 'em."

"Heard you were trying to find me."

"Down this way and thought I could score some dance lessons."

She laughed softly. "Still in Pintler?"

"Just headed north," I said. "It's been a couple of long days."

"Have you eaten?"

"This week?"

"You still like red wine?"

"What year?"

"Picky, huh?"

"Red's my favorite flavor."

I could hear her smiling as she gave me directions to her house.

The place was harder to find than I'd expected. A couple of wrong turns, one dead end that got me almost into a hay barn and night had truly set in by the time I'd found the right road and eased the pickup down a narrow wooded lane to her house. It was a modern-looking single-story affair that seemed to be cut right into a forest of pines. Pat was standing outlined in the light of the open front door.

"That truck of yours makes a pretty good racket," she said as I walked up. "I heard you coming." A gentle teasing smile etched her lips and she took my arm lightly in hers. "Come on in. I've uncorked your favorite."

As she led me into the living room I thought to myself how god-awful my spartan cabin must have looked to her eyes. Her furniture actually matched: a cream-colored sofa and an easy chair braced an antique coffee table inlaid with gold and lapis and set with a bottle of red wine and two delicate crystal glasses. Bare oak floors shone in the soft light and the simple white walls wore a scattering of brightly colored oils that looked almost tropical. There were flowers in the windows and lacy-looking curtains. Beneath it all was the smell of roasting onions or garlic. I heard my stomach growl and silently willed it to shut up.

"We'll eat in a bit," she said with that soft smile. "First, sit." She poured the wine and proposed a toast—to my first visit to her house. She emphasized the word "first." We clinked glasses.

"And here's to Pat Hornick," I offered. "Wait a minute: here's to Pat Gonzalez. May your house be blessed." We clinked glasses again. "Nice house. Matching furniture, huh?"

She laughed at that and we talked about her house. After a while we got around to Woolsey and I brought her up to date on Summey's disappearance. That sent the mood toward a downhill slide that I didn't want.

"Last time we tried dinner," I said, "a kid ruined it. Not going to let a rancher ruin it tonight. What'd you cook?"

"Hope you like enchiladas?" she said with shy eyes.

"Any potted dormice?"

"You're a brute."

"And you're beautiful." We raised our glasses in another toast and I watched as she brought the delicate rim to her lips. They were the same color as the wine. A soft ruby red. She caught my glance and looked away and in the movement a strand of coal-black hair brushed across her eye.

"You look spectacular," I said, softly.

"You look pretty good yourself," said Pat, just as softly. We touched glasses again but this time I took the glass gently from her hand and bent slowly to her lips. They were warm and close with the wine's lingering perfume and I savored them for an instant and we lost ourselves to the mind-emptying intimacy of a moment that knew no boundaries and heard no clock. We came up for air at some point, exchanged a glance and then plunged back in again and again, and yet again, into this new pool we'd discovered in each other's arms. It was like feeding a hunger you didn't know was there.

Suddenly she disentangled and pushed herself up. "Give me a minute," she said, leaving me a long liquid glance and disappearing into a back room. I sat there trying to catch my breath and my wits. Patches of my hair were standing on end, my shirttail had come untucked, I'd somehow lost my boots and I'd discovered a hole in one of my socks. Like a small tornado had hit me. Then I heard her voice and she was next to me again, and in my arms.

When I opened my eyes the next morning she was gone. A note was propped up on the kitchen table: breakfast which was last night's dinner was in the oven, the coffee was fresh, cowboys could sleep all day but doctors had things to do. She'd signed it "With Love, Pat."

NINETEEN

SUMMEY'S DISAPPEARANCE should have given a new urgency to things: Summey gone, ten billion in gold lying up there in the mountains, Carson still dead. There should have been a new urgency as I drove back to my place after the night at Pat's, but I mostly wasted the rest of the day. I suppose I got a little work done. I finally found the realtor on the phone and left her checking out Joe Summey's ranch. I called Bowen to let him know I was still among the living but his new computer had arrived and he didn't have a lot of time for idle chat, as he put it.

I called Sante Fe directory assistance but there was no Joe Summey in the book. I tried the newspaper but they'd never heard of him. A guy there gave me the names of a couple of art galleries but they drew just as big a blank when I mentioned Summey's name. I also called John Hunt and got him on the Summey scent. But beyond that I didn't do much beyond arranging with a flower shop in Hamilton for a dozen roses to be sent to Pat at the clinic.

Her face had filled the drive home. And that afternoon as I did the usual chores around the place and tried to think at least a little about Carson Woolsey, I kept feeling her touch on my arm as we walked into the house, her soft voice during the night. I almost drove back to Pintler but when I called the clinic they said she was out on an emergency and they didn't know when she'd get back.

I was asleep when she finally called, groping up out of the darkness to try to get the cellphone to work. The miserable thing.

"Ben?" Her voice sounded thin and uncertain on the line.

"Hi Pat." Did mine sound as uncertain going back?

"They said you called?"

"Checking in," I said. "How are you?"

"Sorry, but I had a nasty farm accident on my hands. Just got home."

"Bad?"

"Real bad. The guy got his intestines mixed up in the power takeoff on a tractor."

"Alive?"

"Barely."

"Sorry."

"Thanks, Ben. Yeah, not much of a day." I could hear her lighting a cigarette in the background. "I put some feelers out on Summey."

"Feelers?"

"I've talked to some people. If he surfaces at all we should know it."

"Thanks."

Her voice softened. "I see you found the breakfast?"

"Cowboys can sleep all day but doctors are busy?"

A pause on the line, then: "The roses are lovely, Ben."

"You got 'em?"

"I put them on the coffee table. The whole house smells of roses."

"Nice house."

"I had a nice time," said Pat, shyly.

"Me too."

"I just wanted to..." but she was interrupted by a beeping in the background. "Hold on a minute." I heard her fumbling around and the beeping stopped. She came back on the line. "I hate pagers more than death. I have to go, Ben. Nine-one-one from the office. That means trouble."

"Gotcha," I said. "And Pat, thanks for last night. Let's make sure it's not the last night."

"Me too, Ben. If you don't call me, I call you."

I drifted off again thinking about Pat and was purely and thoroughly asleep the next time the phone went off. And people wonder why I don't like phones.

"Tripp," I growled into the plastic machine.

"Hunt," said the voice on the other end. "You awake?"

"Am now. What time is is?"

"I've been in the library," said Hunt.

"And?"

"And, I got two or three things that might be interesting."

I sat up and switched on the reading light. The clock said two a.m. "Such as?"

"First off, there's no record of any activity up in the Sula Basin area for the last ten, fifteen years."

"Activity?" My mind was still heavy with sleep.

"Exploration. Sometimes you have to get a license from the state, depends on the claim situation. But there's no license."

"And that means what?"

"I don't know what it means," said Hunt. "But I found some other stuff."

"Other stuff?"

"Yeah. I figured maybe we could come in the back door on this thing. Find out who's licensed to process gold in the state and start running down that list."

"And what'd you find?"

"That it'd be a lot of work. State records show more than four hundred companies. Man, I didn't think there'd be anything like that number. Four hundred companies out there working gold claims. I didn't think there was that much gold in Montana."

"Gordon Technology in there?"

"Nope."

"You get the list?"

"I copied it off," said Hunt. "And something else. It looks like your friend Summey may have misled you about one little thing." I could hear a smile behind the statement.

"Like…?"

"Like you said his name was Joe, right?"

"Joe Summey. Right."

"And he had a place in Sante Fe?"

"That's what he said."

"Ever hear of a painter named Jeremiah Summey?"

"Jeremiah?"

"Jeremiah Summey," said Hunt.

"The guy I know is named Joe."

"Well, the guy I found is named Jeremiah Summey. But it sounds like the same character. I found one of his exhibitions." Pride in the statement.

"Exhibitions?"

"I got some help from a friend in the art department," said Hunt, "and we dug into the stacks to see what might be there. Sure enough we found a couple of things about this guy Jeremiah. Some of his stuff was for sale in an old catalogue. Nothing pricey. They had one thing in there by Summey that they described as a mountain landscape, wanted two hundred and fifty bucks for it.''

I pictured Summey painting in his living room and talking about being discovered by, as he put it, the foo-foo crowd in Sante Fe. Two hundred fifty dollars for a painting wouldn't pay that kind of rent. ''Two hundred fifty dollars?'' I asked. ''Sure it's not two hundred and fifty thousand dollars?''

''Nope, two hundred and fifty smackolas.''

''You said exhibition?''

''Yup. Houston.''

''Houston as in Texas?''

''No, New Jersey. Of course Texas. The ad talked about two dozen works by a renowned Western land-scape artist''—Hunt laughed—''that's what they called him, 'a renowned Western landscape artist.' There's a short bio on him talking about a couple of other exhibitions he's had. All in Houston. It described him as a true son of the West who now splits his time between his ranch in Montana and the Gulf Coast.''

''No mention of Sante Fe?''

''None. Everything's Houston.''

''And he had exhibitions there?''

''Looks like he had a couple around the city. Nothing current but he's been down there. Does this stuff help?''

''You bet,'' I said into the phone. ''And, John, thanks.''

I got up and checked the lock on the door and peered out the window for a time. The horses were gathered under the eaves of the barn. The night seemed quiet.

EARLY THE NEXT MORNING I took a ride to the West-lands office, a squat two-story building under the main runway by the airport. The building was still locked up tight but a wire gate that led to the rear was open and I wandered through. A line of tractors was ranked up under a large open-faced shed. In the building next door, a guy was welding something on a green and yellow John Deere baler. Beyond, I could see a couple of white pickups, two big harvesting machines, a large flat-bed trailer, and a couple of gasoline pumps. I was headed over to talk to the guy when Roberta pulled up. She came out of her car smiling and gave me an air kiss on the cheek.

"You get the wine?" she asked, beaming. Her blond dark hair was pulled back in a bun and she was decked out in a loose white shirt and tight jeans. "I left it on the table."

"Got it," I said. "Thanks. I was out fishing. Sorry I missed you."

"Me too. I had a whole empty evening. Maybe we can try it again one of these days?" The look in her blue eyes was unmistakably inviting and I was instantly regretting that afternoon fishing trip into the mountains. If I'd just stayed home.

"I've got the wine on ice," I lied. "Next time give me a call before you make that long drive."

"I did. A message said your phone was basically turned off."

"Right." Stupid phone.

"So what brings you out so early? Want to rent out that beautiful place of yours or something?"

I grinned. "I don't know if you guys could handle it, that herd of wild horses and all."

"I saw them in the field. Pretty horses."

"And bears," I added.

"Bears?"

"One came by for a visit the night you left the wine."

A look of concern in her eyes. "You didn't get hurt or anything?"

"The little guy was on a tulip raid. I shooed him away. I actually came by this morning on business. You have time to talk?"

"Always," she said. "Follow me."

The woman led me through a back door into the building and down a narrow corridor to her office. It was a large corner room that looked out on the equipment yard. A matter-of-fact metal desk, metal filing cabinets, and a couple of hard straight-backed chairs of the sort you'd expect at a PTA meeting.

"So what's on your agenda?" asked Roberta, settling behind the desk. "Anything new on Woolsey?"

I shook my head. "Nothing really new on the car wreck but maybe something else. You remember, the last time we talked I mentioned some construction I'd found up in the hills behind the ranch?"

"Right," she said. "And I checked with our foreman and he didn't know anything about it."

"Well, I did some more checking on it," I said. "It turns out there's been quite a bit of activity up there, more than just that one meadow. Two places, actually, on Woolsey's property. And a third place—it's on the ranch next door."

"The same thing?"

"Not really construction," I said. "Places where someone's been in with heavy equipment. Exploring for gold."

"Gold! You mean gold as in jewelry gold? Gold gold?" A look of astonishment on her face.

"Gold gold," I said. "It looks like most of the work happened last summer, but it's strange—somebody— came in and covered over one of the sites in the last week or two. That ring any bells?" I watched her face closely for any hint of what might be going on behind her eyes. There wasn't much beyond surprise. If anything, maybe there was a little too much surprise…but that might just be her character. I realized I hardly knew the woman.

"Covered over one of the sites?" she said.

"Filled it in and covered it with topsoil."

"That's not us, not Westlands. I mean, that's just basically not us, Ben. You think that happened in the last week?"

"In the last week or so. Nothing like that, huh?"

"Nothing," she said. "After we talked I asked our guy down there to keep me up to date on anything we did. There's been nothing. I mean, we're way behind schedule. We should have started some of the soil preparation for the grain fields but we haven't gotten to it yet, we're just so far behind."

"And nothing from last summer? That's when most of the work went on. Last summer?"

"Nothing. Remember? I checked with our foreman and there was nothing like that." Her eyes were still wide. "You're talking about real gold? Like the stuff rings are made of?"

"That's the stuff. Ever hear of a company called Gordon Technology?"

"Gordon Technology?"

I nodded.

"Should I? What is it?"

"A name that's come up."

"I can ask around."

"And there's nothing going on up on the ranch?"
I eyed the cabinets behind her. "Anything in the
files?"

"I doubt it."

"Maybe we could look?"

"They're private company documents."

"And an old man's dead."

Reluctantly she pulled a large ring-bound file from
one of the metal cabinets.

"You mind?" I asked, moving around to look over
her shoulder.

"It's confidential stuff."

"I don't tell secrets."

"I'm trusting you," she said and opened the Woolsey file. The first items were a copy of the original
deed to the ranch and the Westlands contract signed
by somebody from the company and Carson Woolsey
and dated roughly six years before. A boiler-plate contract: Westlands takes over ranch operations and pays
Carson Woolsey back 33 percent of profits and ab-
sorbs any losses itself. A thick stack of pages detailing
equipment and property on the ranch and a survey
showing the legal boundaries. The file also contained
an old county plat map which showed the major dwell-
ings, the streams and roads, even the abandoned
mines.

"You ever see that?" I asked pointing to the mines.

"I haven't actually studied this file before," Roberta said. "Just skimmed it."

We continued paging through but the rest of the file
was mostly sales receipts and work orders for planting

and harvesting—nothing about any construction—or exploration—on the property whatsoever.

Roberta closed the files and I sat back down.

"No other files or documents?"

She shrugged. "I'm afraid that's it. The whole thing. But it sure raises some issues." Roberta wrote a note on a desk calendar. "We're going to have to investigate this, I mean we, Westlands. If somebody's working up there without our permission, they're breaking the law. Have you taken this to the sheriff?"

"Not yet."

"Okay, I'll need to pull in some people from our corporate office, people with some experience in this kind of thing. Any ideas on your part? You have any guesses who might have been in there?"

"Nothing I can take to a grand jury yet."

Roberta rose and it was obvious our meeting was over. "Let me get on this, Ben. Maybe there's something we can do. I'll call you." She squeezed my arm in her hand. "We'll still have that bottle of wine, huh?"

Back in the pickup I called the clinic and managed to get Pat but her tone was way down.

"What's wrong?"

"He died."

"The farmer?"

"During the night. I went up to Hamilton but he was dead by the time I got to the hospital. I spent the rest of the night with his wife…and his kids."

"That's a tough one." I didn't know what else to say.

"Got a pencil?" said Pat.

I rummaged in the glove box. "Got one."

"Then take this down," she said and gave me the

name and address of a shop called Dufour's and a telephone number with a 713 area code. Houston.

"Summey?"

"Summey," said Pat. "I got to thinking: Summey's a painter, right? How do you ship paintings? Courier service, right? So there's this woman I treated once—works at a courier service up in Hamilton. I called her. She thought the name sounded familiar right off the bat and looked back in her receipts. Summey shipped with them three or four times."

"Pictures?"

"Probably. Large and fragile."

"Ties in with what Hunt found," I said. "Looks like Summey had some exhibitions in Houston. How recent was the last receipt?"

"Last fall," said Pat. "I hope the trail's not too cold."

"Yeah." I paused for a moment. "I'm sorry about the farmer."

"Me too, Ben. You're going down there, aren't you?"

"Looks that way."

"Stay safe."

"I promise."

I tried the 713 number. A woman's voice: "Dufour's, may I hep you?"

"This isn't the airport?"

"It's Dufour's Gallery, sir."

"I'm sorry. I was trying to get the airport. You're a gallery?"

"'Fraid so."

"Pictures, things like that?"

The woman chuckled. "Things like that."

"Well, I might stop by," I said, putting as much

flirt into my voice as I thought I could get away with. "What part of town you in?"

The woman gave me directions, a small flirt beginning to surface in her own voice.

I hung up promising to visit. I couldn't risk asking her if she had any Summeys. If he heard about it, my chance of ever finding him would be gone.

TWENTY

HOUSTON ASSAULTED ME like a giant greenhouse as I stepped out of the terminal at Hobby Field—hot, muggy, smelly. The pungent odor of jet fuel mingled with the subterranean scent of rotting vegetables to give the air an almost palpable feel of the Third World. Huge thunderheads were gathering to the west as I collected a rental car and made my way through the agonizing crawl of afternoon rush toward Dufour's gallery.

The sun disappeared and the clouds let loose by the time I got there: a torrential frenzy of rain slashing almost horizontally along the streets; cars throwing up rooster tails of spray from their tires, lightning cracking like a chorus of heavy artillery.

I pulled up across the street from the gallery and let the motor run, the wipers slapping like a spongy metronome to some underwater ballet.

Dufour's wasn't much to look at from the outside: a broad window with a couple of framed paintings displayed in it, a narrow door, subdued lights inside. A woman was sitting at a desk but no one else seemed to be around. I wondered if she was the one I'd flirted with. At length the clouds drifted on and the sun came back. I killed the motor and crossed the street.

The woman looked up with a mercantile smile as I

pushed through the door. Forty-something, chunky plastic jewelry, henna-red hair, a shapeless brown dress. "Evening," she drawled in a deep-Texas accent. It wasn't the voice I'd heard on the phone. "Terrible weather, huh?"

I returned her smile. "Managed to avoid it." The room was long and narrow. On one white-washed wall they'd hung probably a half dozen oil paintings, each illuminated by its own small spotlight. Portraits, mostly—and mostly crude. I marvelled that people might actually spend money on such stuff. The other wall held landscapes: mountains in heavy earth colors, terracotta deserts, electric-blue lakes. One painting toward the end of the row caught my eye. I'd seen those colors before. Blue sky, brown earth. And I'd seen those mountains before—looking out Joe Summey's window. Bingo. A small private moment of victory. I didn't need to look for the signature to know the painter, but it was there. Jeremiah Summey. "Nice work," I said casually. "Local?"

The woman came around from behind her desk and joined me in front of the painting. "We're so proud of his work," she said. "Jeremiah Summey. Quite a reputation. Are you a collector?"

I pretended to study the picture, as though I actually knew something about art. Maybe it fooled her, maybe it didn't.

"Summeys are *tres* collectible these days," she said, her voice taking on a small edge of retail intensity. "A lovely quality about it, don't you think? I mean, it's like he gives you the mountain, not just a painting of a mountain. Do you collect?"

"Actually, I was walking down the street and just

happened to drop in. What's his name again?" I looked at a price tag: Four hundred dollars.

"Jeremiah Summey. He lives on a ranch in Montana, can you imagine? And paints what's around him. What a lovely place it must be."

We both stood back and surveyed the wall of paintings. I recalled Summey talking about their rustic quality. He had it right: I'd seen stuff like this in some of the most rustic motels in America.

"Montana, huh?" I said. "Long way from home?"

"Actually, it's Montana and Houston. He spends a lot of his time down here. I think he has a boat on the Gulf."

"Nice way to live. Is he around? I'd like to meet him, I mean, if that sort of thing's possible?"

"Sure," she said. "You just missed him. But he said he'd drop by in the morning. Maybe you could come back?"

"Understand," I said. "Maybe tomorrow."

I got myself a couple of Dr. Peppers, some Mexican take-out, and a cheap motel and settled in to wait for The Artist Formerly Known as Joe.

IT WAS HOT the next morning, Houston baking under a robin-egg sky and the locals already beginning to show signs of that glassy-eyed daze you see in climates too hot for people to live in. I found an unobtrusive spot for the rental car well down and across the street from the gallery. I left the motor on and the air conditioner running and waited.

Half a block down an ice house was beginning to catch a few early-morning customers, day laborers mostly, men in tee shirts and baggy shorts sliding in for a cold breakfast beer. Just across from me, an enormously fat woman in a tent-like dress in a faded flower pattern was slowly going through the process of getting a taco stand ready for business.

A little before eleven, the woman from the day before showed up and let herself through the front door of the gallery.

It was shortly after two when I finally saw my man. Summey was climbing out of a new BMW roadster directly in front of the gallery. I was almost startled by how familiar he seemed: the same ponytail of grey hair, the boxer's wide frame, the ageless face. He had on a faded red tank top, baggy light-colored cotton trousers, and sandals. He looked tanned and fit and I had to remind myself again that I was dealing with a man in his 70s.

It couldn't have been more than fifteen minutes before Summey came out, got in the car, and pulled away. I slid into traffic a couple of cars back and followed. Just this side of downtown, he shot up an entrance ramp onto the freeway that heads east toward Galveston and the Gulf. Summey moved to the fast lane and we made good time: I saw the exit for the airport, after a while another exit for a naval air station and then we were in flat open country, the city fading away behind us. After half an hour we came on a sign marked NASA ROUTE 1 and Summey pulled into the exit lane and turned off. I stayed with him about a quarter mile back.

After that I'm not sure where we went. I saw the Johnson Space Center with its techno playground of derelict rockets at one point. We crossed over a river or wide inlet on a tall bridge with Galveston Bay stretching out beyond, small whitecaps erupting across its muddy face. A few more jabs and hooks of traffic and Summey pulled into a large open parking lot. Beyond, a forest of masts sprouted from a marina.

I stayed in my car as Summey unloaded a couple of grocery bags onto a cart, locked up his car, and pushed the cart toward the harbor. Beyond were maybe two hundred boats, sailboats mostly, though there were a few big power boats—cabin cruisers—sprinkled in the lot.

Summey paused at the foot of a ramp to enter some numbers into a combination lock. A wire mesh gate swung open and he pushed his cart onto a long finger-like floating wooden pier and made his way to a large white sailboat. It was a nice boat: probably 40 or 42 feet on deck, sloop-rigged with a tall aluminum mast, a smart-looking bowsprit pointed off the nose, teak trim along the sides, a blue sail cover printed in white with the name "Big Sky." Joe—or Jeremiah—Summey seemed to be doing just fine in the finance department, pretty good for a rancher who had borrowed himself in over his head and had to auction off his equipment.

I watched from my car as Summey opened the cabin hatch and disappeared below with the groceries. He came out a few minutes later and fussed with something in the rear cockpit for a while. At length he went below again and this time pulled the cabin hatch closed behind him.

I found a place to park that gave me a good view of the pier and of Summey's boat and settled down to wait. After a while a nice-looking boat motored past and I forgot all about Joe Summey. A Bristol Channel Cutter. I'd almost bought one once: just 28 feet on deck but heavy-built for blue water. A boat that could circumnavigate, a salty little boat. The ad had said she was in Bristol condition. A Bristol Bristol and I'd come very close to owning her. Now I sat remembering the lust I'd had for that little boat and the freedom from tedium she'd promised at the time—and wondering where I'd be right that minute if I'd bought a circumnavigator instead of inheriting a ranch in the Montana mountains. I thought of Pat, too, and wondered if she liked to sail, wondered idly if I could get her out of the doctor's smock long enough to try it. Then the blue eyes and blond hair of Roberta nudged into the reverie so I dressed her in a tiny bikini and put her on the foredeck of the new boat I'd buy when I sold the ranch and decided it was an image worth thinking about for a while.

It was seven o'clock exactly when Summey left for dinner. I'd somehow missed him getting off the boat, spotting him only as he was passing through the mesh gate: white trousers this time, a blue blazer over a colored shirt. He climbed into his car and sat there for a minute or two as the machine automatically stowed the convertible top. He did a broad circle out of the lot and headed my way down the road. Again, I let him get a good distance beyond before I pulled in to follow. I needn't have bothered. After only half a mile he turned off into a paved drive that led through a large ornate gate. I cruised by: a sign etched into the stone pillar said BLUEWATERS YACHT CLUB, MEMBERS ONLY.

There was no place that I could park and watch without standing out like a duck in a punch bowl or getting run over by a drunken fisherman so I cruised back to the marina to wait. The sun went down with an impressive orange and crimson sky show and cabin lights started winking on across the harbor. A gentle breeze had sprung up and the rigging on the masts began to softly peal like a rich man's wind chimes. I could make out a couple of people sitting on their boats in the darkness. Somebody was barbecuing and a shower of sparks drifted up into the night. A crack of laughter in the dark.

Summey made it home at 10:45, a little worse for wear apparently. I saw his car come in, the top up this time, and watched as he made his way unsteadily across the lot to the ramp, his form washing in and out of the pale street lights. He seemed to have troubles with the combination at the gate but finally made it through and walked gingerly down the wooden pier, staggering at one point as it moved slightly in the wash of the tide. He had a few more problems navigating the side of his own boat but eventually made it on. I lost him in the darkness of the cockpit but after a while a dim light came on below. I waited maybe five minutes before it went out and the boat was swallowed back into the darkness.

I circled once through the parking lot, checking to make sure that Summey was well and truly down for the night, and then headed off to find a motel. If he left once, I knew, he'd leave again—and when he did I'd be ready.

TWENTY-ONE

I MADE PREPS the next morning for the coming evening. It wasn't much, really: at one of those big discount places I picked up a cheap blue blazer, a flashlight, and a bottle of wine. At a hardware store I found a set of bolt cutters and a small can of compressed liquid nitrogen and then retired to the motel to kill time. The day dragged and I phoned Bowen but he didn't have much to offer beyond the news that his new computer was up and running and that Hunt had dropped by with a list of the mining companies.

I called Pat at the clinic but she was with a patient. I thought about calling Roberta but realized I didn't have anything particularly to say and the whole thing would be awkward. I considered going for a swim but when I called the desk to ask about local beaches, the guy started laughing out loud. That kind of day: too wired to relax and not one thing I could do about it.

A patch of thunderstorms washed through early evening as I put together my gear, slipped on the blazer, and cruised to the marina. Summey's car was parked in the lot and his boat looked battened down tight with no signs of life. A couple of sailboats glided past down the canal, off for an evening cruise on the bay. On one a knot of maybe ten people were drinking and laughing and I felt a quick pang of loneliness.

At eight o'clock Summey materialized on the back of his boat, dressed again in his blue blazer and snappy trousers. I watched as he made his way up the dock and across the parking lot to his car and pulled away. This time he went right on past the gates to the yacht club and my spirits sank: my plans to be a burglar wouldn't work if I couldn't predict his movements. After about two miles he pulled off into the driveway of a high-rise apartment house that fronted the bay. I coasted to a stop across the road and watched as he disappeared into the building. After a while he came out with a woman on his arm. I couldn't see her face but she was nearly as tall as he, thin, young-looking.

I worried for two miles that they were headed back to his boat, but Summey instead turned into the yacht club. I slowed as his car disappeared through the gates, then hit the gas pedal: time for this rancher to go yachting.

Summey's marina was dark as a felony as I drove in. The sailboats were rocking gently on a rising tide and dim lights winked from the cabins here and there. Like the night before, a soft breeze had kicked up and the harbor was gently noisy with wire rigging chiming against metal masts and the soft grunt and hiss of stretched rope. I was feeling a bit like that rope myself: tied up and tight, my pulse racing, my palms sweating. I wondered briefly if I was having a malaria attack and then smiled to myself at the thought.

I tucked the bolt cutters and flashlight into my pocket, straightened my blazer, and walked down toward the wire gate as casually as I could, the bottle of wine in one hand, the small can of gas hidden in my other. About halfway down the ramp a couple materialized out of the darkness. We exchanged pleasant "howdys" and it seemed as though they'd seen me with my wine and over-dressed blue blazer for what I hoped to seem—a landlubber showing up for his big date on a boat.

At the gate I palmed the small can of liquid nitrogen and hit the combination lock with a shot of its freezing cold spray. The metal shattered with a sudden sharp crack, falling in pieces into the water below. I looked around: no one to hear or see it. I pushed the gate open and walked casually down the dock. Maybe a hundred yards along I heard noises from the cockpit of a large power boat. A couple was doing some very human things in the shadows and certainly didn't notice me. I left the bottle of wine on their stern.

At Summey's boat I did a quick 360 to check for company and then swung aboard, dropping into the deep dark in the bottom of the cockpit. I crouched there for fully two minutes, letting my eyes adjust to the darkness and my ears to the sounds around. To the rear a small red light shone in the engine control panel. Above that the stainless steel steering wheel reflected the lights from the parking lot. Along either side I could make out white fiberglass benches moulded into the hull, a couple of large winches, and some coils of rope. In front, a heavily varnished hatch cover with a solid padlock at the top. All around the smell of salt water and diesel. Beyond my small corner of darkness the sounds of the marina seemed uninterrupted by my silent presence.

I pulled out the bolt cutters and set their steel jaws against the padlock, stripping off my jacket and wrapping it around the cutters to muffle any noise. With a quick scan all around I snapped the lock: I could barely hear it myself as it gave. I dropped the pieces over the side, pulled the hatch open, and scuttled inside, closing it behind me.

Under the beam of the small flashlight I oriented myself quickly. To one side I could make out a galley with a stainless steel stove set on gimbals, a row of drawers, a double sink with a brass faucet. To the other side, a small navigation table with more drawers. Behind me a closed door that would lead rear to a sleeping compartment under the cockpit. I swept the light carefully forward and could make out a large central salon with upholstered benches over storage compartments, a polished wooden table in the middle. Further forward another door that would lead, probably, to a toilet and then another sleeping compartment. An air conditioner hummed somewhere.

I pulled the curtains closed over the portholes and with the narrow beam of the flashlight shielded in one hand started going through the navigation table. Nothing remarkable in the first drawer: charts, some small electronic gear, a flare gun, some audio tapes, a diving knife. In the second drawer more of the same and a leather-bound ship's log. I skipped the first part and opened it to the last few entries. Records of routine maintenance and a few trips out into the bay, guests that had been on board—the names meant nothing to me—a few cursory entries for the weather. Not much of a log. I skimmed back through a half inch of pages and more of the same. The first page, though, held a little gem: Summey had written in long-hand in blue ink "To this new life and this new ship, Big Sky, may you have calm seas and following winds." It was dated almost exactly four years before. The same time his neighbor's ranch had suddenly gone on the market and had just as suddenly been withdrawn, the same time the militia boys had been told to get lost, the same time men had come out and packed their pockets with rocks from that remote stretch of Montana mountain. I stowed the log and went through the rest of the drawers. Nothing revealing—hose clamps, candles, repair receipts, all things related directly to the boat. I needed things related directly to that other part of Summey's life.

I was halfway through the kitchen drawers when I heard voices outside and flattened, killing the light and freezing in the blackness. A man and a woman talking, the voices drawing near. The woman laughed about something, a high tinny laugh that for some reason terrified me. They must have leaned against the boat— I felt it rock slightly. There was silence for a minute and then their voices were fading as they apparently walked away down the pier. I brought my breathing back under control, wiped my palms, checked my watch: nearly 9:30. I had to hurry.

I finished the galley, finding nothing. The front sleeping area had drawers stuffed with clothes. A hanging locker, or closet, was filled with slacks, a couple of coats, spare bedding. I prized the mattress up to get at the compartments below: life jackets, snorkelling gear, fishing tackle.

I worked my way methodically through the storage compartments under the benches in the main salon. More boating stuff but not the kind of personal Summey-related things I needed. The same again as I searched through the rear sleeping compartment. That was obviously where Summey made his home: I found an alarm clock, underwear, a shaving kit, things like that, domestic things. But nothing that helped me fig-

ure this guy out—figure out, for instance, where the
money came from to afford this floating palace.

And time was running out. It was past ten now. I
sat down in the darkness of the main salon and tried
to collect myself. I'd searched through every storage
compartment and drawer I could imagine on the boat
and had found nothing beyond the entry in the log
book...no personal papers of any kind. But they had
to be around, unless—and my heart sank with the re-
alization—unless Summey had some sort of storage
compartment on land. The more I thought about it, the
more sense it made: you can't reasonably live on a
boat the way you do on dry land. And he'd had a
house full of furniture and personal items in Montana.
Unless he'd sold them off, he'd had to store them
somewhere. That was it. And that was a tough one to
crack: there was no way of knowing when or even if
he'd visit a storage area. I could spend a summer, or
a lifetime, waiting for that and not get any closer to
the truth. I did a mental kick to my own head for not
considering it before I'd sent myself off on this chase
to Houston. I'd have to regroup, think of something.

A quick scan around the salon again with my flashlight. I hadn't missed anything, or if I had it was hidden cunningly enough that I couldn't find it. I checked
the rear sleeping compartment again to make sure I
left it as I had found it and then went forward and did
the same there. In the salon, I pulled back the curtains
and rehooked them. And was moving toward the rear
hatch when just the softest glint of light bounced up
from the deck. I paused—that errant firing of a neuron
again, the seeds of a hunch, of an intuition.

I turned on the flashlight and dropped down to my
knees. A small brass thumb latch shone dully from the

teak and holly of the wooden deck. Popping it open
with both hands, I pulled up the floor hatch and trained
the light down into the bilge. Some hosing and a couple of circular faucets, a sealed electric junction box—
and a solid grey plastic container the size of a small
suitcase. I undid the clasp and pulled back the lid: a
thick row of neatly indexed files. Summey's papers. I
held the flashlight in my mouth and scanned the tabs
quickly. One read BOAT, another CAR, still another said
ART. I pulled out a file labeled BANK and paged
through it: a local Texas bank and a number of deposit
records. I tallied them up—Summey was salting away
about $15,000 a month, most of it cash deposits. I
found the latest statement: $1.2 million and change in
savings, $18,000 plus in checking. Jesus. No wonder
he could afford a 42-foot sailboat and a BMW roadster: that was just pocket money for this guy. I scanned
further back through the bank file and found a couple
of money market accounts with several hundred thousand in each of them, more deposit slips, more bank
statements. I pulled out another file marked INVEST-
MENTS and was about to go through it when I noticed
at the back of the case a slim file marked RANCH. I
pulled that out and scanned through it: an old deed
showing his ownership. Then something new I hadn't
seen before. A thick contract by the look of it. Legalese on the first page but two words that seemed to
scream out: *minerals* and *exploration*. My heart
jumped.

Suddenly, outside, more voices. Summey's voice
this time, no doubt about it. A bolt of panic as I clawed
through the papers with one hand even as my other
hand reached for the floor hatch. The voices were
drawing up alongside the boat—almost desperately I

tore though the papers. I felt the boat move ever so slightly. There in the papers. Something called Rainbow Mines.

Suddenly, hands fumbled with the main hatch. I killed the light and crawled frantically toward the bow, scuttling into the darkness of the forward sleeping compartment and closing the door as the hatch swung open behind me.

Summey's voice: "But I locked it. I know I did."

"Bet you didn't." A woman's voice. "Did you have a drink?"

Laughter from Summey. "Maybe one or two."

I wedged myself into a small hole between the wall of the bathroom and the raised foot of the mattress. A hatch in the ceiling above me was dogged shut with brass clamps. A possible escape route.

"Just two drinks?" said the woman.

"Come here, you," said Summey.

I eased the door open: Summey and the woman were embracing in the cockpit, darkness behind them, the slow and steady roll of waves rocking the boat gently from side to side, the soft gurgle of water on the hull. The two came out of the embrace and headed for the main hatch. I closed the door.

I waited maybe five minutes and cracked the door. In the twilit darkness I could make out their forms tangled on the settee, both apparently asleep. I crept back into my cabin and slowly, silently, unscrewed the locks in the ceiling above me and opened the hatch. I pushed my head out into the air and heard their voices from the main salon.

The woman was giggling. "I want to sail."

"Too late to sail," Summey growled.

The little-girl voice: "Please?"

"Too late, and I've had a few. And you wore me out."

"Please?"

Summey laughing. "Okay. But just the motor. I'm too old to sail."

I boosted myself up through the hatch and scrambled out, rolling across the deck to the side rail. Summey's form materialized from inside the boat not twenty feet away, his back to me. I slipped over the rail and silently lowered myself into the water. Summey was bent over the engine controls at the rear of the cockpit. No sign of the woman. I pushed off from the hull and began swimming down the darkened channel toward the lights of the parking lot, checking back over my shoulder from time to time as I silently pushed my way through the black water.

I heard the diesel starter grind once, and then twice—and suddenly every atom of air around me erupted in scalding white-hot light and something smashed across my shoulders and it was like a giant hand was plunging me downward into the choking darkness.

I came to gasping in a great lung-full of salt water. Frantically, I thrashed my arms and legs and after a claustrophobic lifetime my head broke the surface. I vomited out water and drew in sweet air and then vomited again and then managed to start breathing. The night behind me danced red and orange and I dog-paddled around to see the sky and the sea filled with fire and the boat a blazing pyre. I watched in disbelief as the flames ate outward through the fiberglass hull like it was newspaper. A large whoof as a can of propane lit off and the air scalded my face and I ducked back into the waves. When I came up again the boat was already settling fast by the stern. The tall mast tilted back, the pointed bow broke free of the water, and then the whole burning mass seemed to lurch backward and settle on the muddy bottom at an impossible angle.

"Summey!" I yelled. "Summey!" But even as I shouted the name I knew there was no hope anyone would ever answer to that call again. Whoever rigged the bomb had done a surgically effective job: Summey and the secrets of his Montana mountain had been shredded to flotsam in the brown uncaring waters of Galveston Bay. Only one secret had escaped—the name Rainbow Mines. I took one final long look and then started kicking toward a dark and unnoticed landing on the Texas shore.

TWENTY-TWO

THINGS WERE DECIDEDLY tense the next night as I met Pat at Bowen's place. I'd called from Houston to fill her in and ask her to bring her computer to Bowen's to help search for Rainbow Mines. She'd angrily accused me of being careless and then had gotten even angrier when I refused to take it to the police, turning deaf to my arguments that I'd grow old in jail before I could explain my presence on Summey's boat. Her anger became fear when it finally sank in that Summey was dead.

I think we were all a little bit frightened as we met at Bowen's that night. Pat was on me in a tight hug before I'd even climbed all the way out of my pickup.

"Ben," she said, burying her face in my neck. "What's happening?"

"Tough to know," I said, holding her there in the deserted parking lot, Bowen pretending not to watch from the porch.

"And Summey is dead?"

"He has to be. If he's not he's the luckiest man alive."

"Like you," whispered Pat and I felt a shiver pass through her body.

"Let's see what we can find," I said and led her into the light of the porch.

Bowen brought out his new computer as Pat got hers plugged in and running.

"I'm into the Net," she said quietly. "What do you need?"

"Connections," I said.

Bowen let off with a groan.

"Nathan?"

"I think I erased a file."

"Here," said Pat, "let me take a look."

The two of them managed to fool with his computer for a good five minutes, Bowen oblivious to the apologetic glances Pat was throwing me across the table. But it was his back porch.

"I think that's it," said Pat at length. "You have to be careful about alt-delete on that machine."

"Can we get to it?" I said. "So connections. We've got Woolsey, Summey, Gordon Technology, and now something called Rainbow Mines. And we've got one connection—we know from the files I saw that Rainbow Mines is hooked with Summey. First we figure out what a Rainbow Mines is. Pat?"

"The Net's an amazing thing," she said. "Rainbow Mines." Bowen and I stood behind her watching as she guided the computer down through its levels of logic, pushing it through the obviously irrelevant to dig deeper and deeper into the web of meanings and connections buried in its mammoth database.

Bowen wandered off and I sat back down and watched Pat as she worked. Her face was a study in absolute concentration as her fingers played the keyboard and her quick dark eyes devoured the information flashing across the screen. She absently brushed a strand of hair from her face and I found myself dipping into the memory of the night at her house. Even in the harsh light of the porch's naked electric bulb, she had an exotic beauty that seemed to radiate from somewhere way below the level of her skin. At one point she looked up to catch me staring and gave me a shy smile.

Bowen returned and was playing with his own computer by the time Pat looked up again. "There's not much in here," she said. "There's a ton of references to Rainbow Mines. One's even a restaurant chain in Australia. But nothing tying any of them to the two ranches. No hits at all when I put the three of them together. And no clue where our Rainbow actually is or who runs it. Ideas?"

I thought about Summey, the nice boat, the contract shining white in the narrow beam of my flashlight. Rainbow Mines standing out from the legalese. The legalese. A legal contract. Written by lawyers. "Try Rainbow Mines and lawyers."

"Lawyers?" said Pat.

"Maybe it's a way in."

Pat shrugged and entered the new words. The machine thought for a few seconds before coming up with a short list of items. Pat scrolled through them. "'Rainbow Mines and its lawyers announced'... hum...here's one: 'Attorneys for Rainbow Mines filed a countersuit'...don't think that's leading...wait, listen to this: 'Rainbow Mines' legal firm, Keeler, Keeler and Boyd.' I don't know if that's our Rainbow Mines—but there's some lawyers."

"What is it again?"

"Keeler, Keeler and Boyd," Pat was still reading. "Los Angeles, New York, London. Keeler, Keeler and Boyd. Big outfit. Now what?"

"Now cross-reference the lawyers with our ranchers,'' I said, ''with Summey and Woolsey. And try Montana in there, too.''

Pat keyed in the words and waited a few seconds as the machine digested the information and then flashed up a new list. ''Here's a…no that's not anything. Nothing on Woolsey. Summey—ditto. No links there. Let me scan back through. Hum. Nope. Nothing between the lawyers and our ranchers. I'm trying Montana now. Here's something. It's a…no, sorry.''

I got up and paced the porch. Pat continued working the machine. ''Here's a new one,'' she said over her shoulder. ''Keeler, Keeler and Boyd. It's a suit against the State of Montana. Right state. Hum, let's see. It's old. Nineteen seventy-nine. Filed in Helena.'' She paused and read through it. When she spoke again her voice was tight. ''Ben, maybe you want to take a look at this?''

I came up behind her. Bowen stopped playing with his machine and watched from across the table.

''It's a lawsuit over a mineral claim in Montana,'' said Pat, her voice so low it was almost a whisper. ''Keeler, Keeler and Boyd are representing…Gordon Technology.''

I leaned over and read the screen. Keeler, Keeler and Boyd and Gordon Technology. Connected. And Keeler, Keeler and Boyd connected with Rainbow Mines. The same Rainbow Mines in papers on Summey's boat? The same Gordon Technology sending geologists up to the neighboring ranch four years before when it goes up for sale? ''Okay,'' I said, ''if it's the same lawyers, maybe it's the same company. See if Rainbow books back directly into Gordon.''

Pat entered ''Rainbow Mines and Gordon Technology.'' The machine thought about it for only a couple of seconds before producing a new line of entries. Pat pulled up the first one: "'Rainbow Mines' parent company Gordon Technology announced they've finalized a deal for…'" She looked up. "There's the link. Gordon Tech owns Rainbow."

"So the horns do link," I said and leaned back against the porch rail. It was beginning to come clear, to swim out of the lies and the fire and the uncertainty. Rainbow Mines—hiding behind a company called Gordon Technology. Somehow they must have figured out there was gold in the mountains above Sula Basin and had come in and nosed around and then like a snake had sunk down low out of sight. Somehow they'd made a deal in there. And they'd come back in and started depositing cash in Joe Summey's bank account and moving dirt around. Had they shoved an inconvenient Carson Woolsey out of the way? Had Summey been blasted out of the way? Were they the faceless ones who had twice now come after me?

Bowen broke the silence. "I've got that list Hunt dropped off."

I gave him a blank look.

"The list of mining companies?" he said. "The ones licensed to do business in the state?" The big man disappeared into the house, returning in seconds with a slim stack of papers. Now that we knew what to look for it was easy. It was on the fourth page. "RBM, Inc."—that couldn't be anything but Rainbow Mines—"surface and sub-surface mineral extraction, state license LUKSW63UJ. Hamilton, MT." Bingo. I had it. And Hamilton. Not an hour's drive from Pintler. The horns were firming up nicely. But exactly how?

I picked up the cellphone and dialled John Hunt's

number. It rang a long time before an answering machine kicked in.

"John," I said, "it's Ben Tripp and I need some help. Give me a call. You and your friend Vicki need to hook me up with an outfit called Rainbow Mines."

TWENTY-THREE

IT TOOK THREE DAYS to make the deal, three days of
nervous waiting as Vicki Brandon negotiated with
Rainbow about a visit. In the end the key was her
title—Doctor of Geology at the University—and what
I came to discover was a secret of the trade: miners
are almost supernaturally nosy and accommodate that
trait with a tradition of field trips to see what the other
guy's doing. A request for a visit could almost not be
ignored, especially a request from a state university to
a company working under a state license.

We'd argued among ourselves about it for three
days while Vicki tried making the arrangements, Hunt
and Pat pointing out with some passion that if these
people had killed Woolsey or Summey or both—and
attacked me—they'd know precisely who I was and it
was stupid for me to go in. Good arguments—but I
had to do something and do it soon, if I ever wanted
to sleep at night again. And when there are no alter-
natives, the only choice is an easy choice to make.

The gold mine was tucked back in the high mountains about midway between Missoula and Pintler.
From ground level, it looked more like a fortress than
a mine. The actual mine itself was an unimpressive
tunnel disappearing into the shoulder of a hill. Around
it were half a dozen trailer houses and sheds, a large

factory-looking building flanked by huge tanks and a giant pile of gravel and crushed stone probably 30 feet high and the size of three or four football fields put together. The whole place was surrounded by a sturdy-looking steel hurricane fence with razor wire strung over the top.

A guard stopped us at the front gate and radioed ahead as we pulled up in Vicki's ancient battered Volkswagen. After a while a blue pickup appeared and a man in a red hard hat, tee shirt, and khakis stepped out. He gave his name as Orin Gacey and said he was the foreman. The man was of medium height and beefy and took us in with a glance that didn't seem particularly friendly.

Vicki produced a business card and introduced me as a money man interested in a possible minerals investment. I had the sense he knew precisely who I was and didn't like it a bit. Maybe it was just nerves. Gacey showed us where to park the car and led us on foot across the rocky lot toward the mine entrance. Vicki made small talk about other mines she'd visited.

"Hard-rock, huh?" she said as Gacey outfitted us with hardhats with little lights on them. "In deep?"

"Pretty good drift," said Gacey. "We're back about three thousand feet. Good vein that seems to be holding pretty well at about half an ounce." His mood seemed to lighten up as he talked about the rock. "We've got a six percent decline on the vein so it gets to be some heavy hauling. Then we've got a roof of some fairly low-grade deposit that we're bringing out too."

The two walked along talking rock as I lagged behind and surveyed the grounds. One of the trailers I'd seen from beyond the fence looked like an office.

Through its window I could see a couple of computers, a woman working behind a desk, and a wall of filing cabinets. I would have given a small fortune in gold right then to see what was in those cabinets.

Another trailer looked like some sort of lab: gas cylinders and round metal containers were stacked against the wall and a chimney above was giving off an acrid-smelling black smoke. In a shed nearby a man in a hard hat was sorting through a tub of drill bits. Next to that another trailer had an air-conditioning unit droning at one end and a door marked in a yellow skull and crossbones. A sign under it said explosives. I wondered if it was stacked with Hawkin's fertilizer—and my mind jumped back to the boat and the black night erupting white-hot around me.

A big engine started up somewhere from beyond the trailers and the air was suddenly filled with a deep heavy pounding so loud we could barely hear ourselves speak. Gacey shouted that they were crushing rock. Vicki nodded and covered her ears.

A large truck built low to the ground emerged from the tunnel with a load of ore in its bed. We watched as it backed up to the mill and tipped the rock into a wide steel grate in the ground. Gacey gestured to us and we climbed up into the truck's empty bed. He gave the high-ball sign to the driver and we bumped along into the tunnel.

I was immediately blinded by the blackness, with only the lights of the truck showing dimly down the long rock corridor. The roar of the crushing machine subsided behind us as we drew in deeper. Gacey and Vicki switched on the lights on their hard hats and I fumbled with mine, feeling like an amateur and hoping it didn't show too much. Gacey was explaining the geology of the tunnel to Vicki and seemed to have forgotten I was there.

The rock walls hovered dimly bone-white in the truck's lights and I caught snatches of conversation about how they'd had to tunnel through some very heavy basalt to get to the heart of the vein. We moved along in a straight line for what must have been about a quarter of a mile and, though the darkness was disorienting, it felt to me like we were gradually descending all the while. At one point electric lights shone ahead of us and we came to a Y in the tunnel and veered to the left. The other tunnel disappeared into blackness within just a few feet.

Another quarter mile probably—or it could have been ten miles, my judgment was so confused—we hit another Y and forked right this time. After a while I could make out some dim lights ahead in the gloom and the truck slowed and then stopped and we hopped out.

Gacey told us not to touch anything and we fumbled along toward the source of the light, Gacey and Vicki stopping at one point to look at the wall and talk about high-grade. Huge noise now, this time a diesel generator and heavy pounding. At length we emerged into a small cavern-like space in the tunnel where two men were working. One was at the controls of a machine that looked like some sci-fi robot with two big mechanical arms drilling into the rock wall. Another man stood nearby, tending a snaking line of cables that led back to a diesel generator. To one side stood a 50-gallon barrel with a hand-pump in the top. To the other side, four bright yellow sacks of Hawkin's fertilizer.

The men stopped drilling as we came up and the generator instantly backed down to idle.

"Showing some visitors around," said Gacey to the man controlling the big robot. "How's the face?"

"Crumbly, boss," said the man.

"Careful," said Gacey. Both men nodded.

"Pretty fair high-grade right in here," said Gacey, turning to us. "Knockin' out almost an ounce a ton."

"How's stability?" asked Vicki.

"Could be better," said Gacey.

Vicki picked up a rock and slipped it into her pocket.

"We've got two more sites working under this mountain," Gacey offered, "other drifts back from where you saw the forks in the tunnel. Three teams working 'round the clock right now. Good high-grade stuff coming out. It's all we can do to keep up with it outside."

"Preg pond stuff?"

Gacey nodded. "Some big ones. I'll show you on the outside. Seen enough?" We both nodded and Gacey turned to the men. "Watch that face, guys. Don't need any high-grade bodies comin' out of here." The men grinned and turned back to the face. The generator revved up and drowned the small space in noise. We walked back down the dark tunnel to the truck and Gacey signaled to the driver.

Back outside the tunnel, the daylight seemed blindingly bright and the racket from the rock-crushing machine was, if anything, even louder. I saw Vicki say something to me—I saw her lips move—but I couldn't make it out and shrugged. She started to say it again but gave up.

Gacey led us up to the giant flat-topped mound of gravel. Hundreds of sprinklers, like lawn sprinklers almost but larger, were washing back and forth and the air was filled with an odd chemical smell almost like almonds. At that point the crushing machine powered down and we could hear for the first time.

"Noisy sucker," said Vicki.

Gacey nodded: "It's the thing I hate most up here."

Vicki was surveying the mound. "Pretty big pile. How's the recovery?"

"Near ninety percent," said Gacey.

Vicki whistled. "Not bad."

"Your friend looks a little confused," said Gacey, eyeing me.

"This is all new to me, I'm afraid."

"You're on a leach pad." He gestured toward the tunnel. "We bring the ore out of the mine, crush it down to about a quarter of an inch and then pile it up here. Those sprinklers are spraying cyanide."

"Cyanide?"

Gacey nodded. "The cyanide leaches down through the ore here and picks up the gold in solution. We collect it with a drainage system underneath and then pull the gold out. Follow me." He led us back around the pile to a series of liquid-filled pits, each roughly the size of an Olympic swimming pool.

"Preg ponds," said Vicki.

Gacey nodded. "Pregnant with gold. This is where we collect the cyanide that has the gold in it. We wash that through a carbon column to filter out the gold."

The pits were lined with heavy plastic and the dark blue liquid oozed the scent of almonds and acrid metal. "How much gold is in that pond right now?" I asked.

"Let's see," said Gacey. "That solution's gone through about a thousand tons of ore. Pulling out maybe half an ounce a ton. What's that come out to?"

"Five hundred ounces," said Vicki quickly. "A hundred and fifty thousand dollars."

Gacey seemed unimpressed with the numbers. "I suppose that's about right."

"And you drain them how often?" I asked.

Gacey was leading us off toward the trailers and spoke back over his shoulder: "Works out to about a pond a week."

Vicki: "So seven and a half million a year?"

"Sounds about right," said Gacey. "We're a small operation."

"Any other mines going?" asked Vicki, innocently.

If Gacey had something to hide he didn't show it. "We're mostly in Nevada," he said. "A few holdings in the Andes and Alaska."

"Some friends have a line on a bulk operation in Idaho," said Vicki casually. "Volcanic-hosted stuff. You doing anything like that?"

I tried to act like I wasn't paying attention. Volcanic-hosted gold was what we'd found in the Sula Basin. If the connection meant anything to Gacey, he didn't show it.

"Interesting technology," he said. "You couldn't have done it a few years ago. They didn't even teach it when I went to school. We've got a couple of pit operations like that going in Nevada. I could arrange a visit if you want it?"

"Might take you up on that," said Vicki.

"Like to show you something else," said Gacey, leading us to the trailer with the gas cylinders and the hoses in the wall.

"Assay lab," said Gacey, undoing a padlock and gesturing us inside. It was a narrow room, windowless, and packed with a hi-tech assortment of digital scales, laptop computers, test tubes, beakers of colored liquid, and what looked like some sort of autoclave or small furnace.

"This is what it all comes down to," said Gacey, picking up a glass vial and holding it up to the light. "The final product." He stared at it for a long minute and then passed it over to me.

The vial was about the size of a jelly jar and surprisingly heavy. It was packed almost to the rim with a fine yellow sand that gave off the soft dull sheen of metal. Gold. I held it in my hands and stared at it with thinly concealed amazement. Two, maybe three pounds of pure gold.

"Dust from the processing," said Gacey. "We smelt it down into ingots before we send it out. Paydirt."

There's something about gold, I thought as I stood there holding it, something almost primeval in its elemental attraction. Gold's not like money, not like a wad of bills. It's something more fundamental, more magnetic to the human soul. I looked at the jelly jar and could begin to imagine how men could sacrifice everything for these little burnished flakes of metal. The prize of a lifetime. Or the prize of death. I handed it back reluctantly.

"Gets you, doesn't it?" Gacey said, almost grimly, and I nodded.

Back outside, Gacey carefully locked the door before leading us across the lot toward the gate. On the way we passed the trailer with the computers and the woman working behind the desk.

"Your headquarters?" asked Vicki.

"Offices," said Gacey and he gave me an odd, almost challenging look. "It's where we keep the family secrets."

I returned the look and I swear at that point we both knew the game: maybe it was paranoia but it seemed to me that what passed between us in that glance had little to do with mining and a lot to do with an old man in a ditch.

Vicki caught the exchange and threw me a furtive glance. Turning back to Gacey she pointed at a trailer that had a skull and crossbones painted in bright yellow on its door. "Blast shack?"

Gacey pulled his gaze away from me and back to her. "Our blast shack," he said neutrally.

"I saw the fertilizer when we were in the tunnel," said Vicki, all innocence. "Is it all ammonium nitrate or do you use some dynamite?"

"We use some dynamite for the tunnel work," said Gacey with another odd look in my direction. "We use plastics, too, for the small controlled stuff. But it's all nitrate for the bigger areas. It's a lot cheaper." He paused like he was thinking about something and then looked me directly in the eyes. "We use ammonium nitrate a lot—depends on what the job is." I felt my breath shorten: beyond doubt Gacey knew what this masquerade was all about.

Nothing more was said as we made our way back to the main gate.

Back in the car and safely away from Gacey, Vicki gave me a sideways wide-eyed stare. "Okay brother," she said, "was that what I thought it was?"

I nodded next to her. "I think it was."

"He all but admitted it right there," she said.

"Seems that way."

"I can't believe he did that," said Vicki. "I mean,

what was that all about? It's like he's inviting you to come in and take a look or something."

"I think he might be," I said. "The question is, why?"

TWENTY-FOUR

IT WAS LATE AFTERNOON by the time I made my way home. Pat's car was parked outside the cabin. She came running out and locked me in a tight frightened hug as I drove up.

"What is it?" I asked, leaning back enough to see her face. It was drawn and pale and her brown eyes were serious.

"You're okay?" she said.

"I'm okay." I felt her shudder in my arms. "Hey girl, I'm fine. Take it easy."

She buried her face in my shoulder. "I think they came after me." Her words hit me like somebody touching a live nerve.

"Came after you?"

"I need to sit down," she said, leaning hard into me.

I led her into the cabin and put her on the edge of the bed, splashing some cold water into a double shot of whiskey and handing it to her. "Talk to me, Pat."

Her hands were trembling slightly as she took the glass. "I couldn't reach you so I came up here. Then you weren't around." Her words were coming out fast. "The sheriff called me and there was somebody at the house and then..."

"Whoa Pat. You gotta slow this down."

She took a drink of the whiskey and seemed to will herself back under control. "I kept thinking they'd done something to you. It scared me to think they'd done something to you."

"I'm okay. Somebody was at your house?"

She nodded. "I left for work the usual time—early—but I'd forgotten my computer. I don't forget things but I'd forgotten my computer so I turned around and when I came back there was a car parked at the head of the lane. I guess I didn't think much about it but then the front door was unlocked and sort of half pushed open. I don't scare easily but with everything that's happened, I'm careful. I mean you have to be careful, right? So I looked around the corner of the door and there was a man standing there inside my house." Pat shuddered and took another long drink of the whiskey.

"You saw a man standing there?"

"It was just a dark shape but it was a man."

"What was he doing?"

"Just standing there. Inside my house."

"Who was it?"

"I don't know."

"He see you?"

"He had to. I ran to my car. But then I decided nobody scares me off my own place. I grabbed a big tree branch and went back there but he was gone."

"You went back there? With a guy in your house?"

Pat was nodding. "Nobody does that to me, Ben. Not now, not ever. I'm prepared to fight for what's mine." She said it with a hard look in her eyes.

"And he was gone?"

The nod again. "I came through the front door swinging, ready to take him on but he wasn't there. I looked through the house and then I heard the car start up. The one parked at the head of the lane. He got gone fast. That's when I started worrying about you.''

"You get the license on the car?''

She was shaking her head. "Sorry.''

"What was the guy doing?''

"That's the part that spooked me. He was just standing there, like he was looking at me, but I couldn't see his face.''

"You call the sheriff?''

"No. That's strange too. The sheriff called me. I got to the clinic—you were at the mine so I didn't know where to go so I went to the clinic—and the sheriff called me.''

"For what?''

"He wanted Joe Summey's medical records and was asking who Summey's dentist was.''

"So they must have found the body.''

Pat nodded. "He said there'd been some sort of accident in Houston. A man and a woman had been killed.''

"What else'd he say?''

"Just that there'd been an accident. The woman was somebody local. They thought the other body was Summey's and the sheriff was trying to find dental records.''

"What kind of accident?''

"The sheriff didn't say. But he asked where you were.''

"What'd you tell him?''

"That I didn't know.''

"You tell him about the guy in your house?''

"I thought I'd better talk to you first.''

"He say anything else?''

Pat's eyes seemed hollow. "What's going on?"

I got up and looked out the window, trying to sort things through in my mind. "I think it's coming apart on them. I don't know what or how exactly—yet—but I think things are unravelling, and they're panicking."

"Who's panicking?"

"I don't know. It's gotta be connected with the gold miners, with Rainbow Mines."

"Who though?"

"I don't have names to put to it yet, I mean not many. We met a guy at the mine today, guy named Orin Gacey. If anyone's in it, he is." I told her about the scene with the trailers and Gacey all but inviting me back in.

"Why do you think they're panicking?"

"It has that feel to it," I said. "Figure it's Rainbow Mines and figure they've got some sort of plan to get the whole mountain. Somehow Woolsey's dying plays into that. We know they've got a deal with Summey. Maybe they start getting scared when we show up asking questions. If their deal with Summey gets exposed, somehow the whole thing blows up on them. Maybe they figure out that I'm getting close and they get scared. So they erase him. Summey and the contract go away in a big ball of fire. Nothing left that can trace back to them."

"You think they knew you were on the boat?"

"I've been thinking about that and I don't know. The bomb went off the second time Summey turned on the ignition. If it's a standard car-bomb sort of thing, it's rigged to go the first time the key's turned. Key makes electrical contact and 'boom.' But this was on the second turn. Maybe somebody was watching and did it with remote control. That would mean they knew I was on there. Two for the price of one. Lucky coincidence. Get rid of Summey, get rid of me.''

''Why'd they break into my house?''

''That's a tougher one,'' I said. ''If they're following me, they know I'm hooked up with you. Maybe they're trying to find out if you know anything. Or maybe trying to scare you.''

''They managed.''

''Or maybe planning to kill you.''

Pat looked at me grimly. ''They'd do that?''

''I don't think this crowd cares much anymore who dies.'' I picked up the cellphone and dialed Bowen's number. He sounded rushed. ''Nate, it's Ben. I think Rainbow's running...and killing.''

''That's bad,'' said Bowen down the line, his voice hollow.

''They came after Pat. I don't know how far it's going to go.''

''Is she okay?''

''Fine. She went after them with a log and they split.''

A small chuckle from the big man. ''Good woman. What's your plan?''

''In their face,'' I said.

''Risky.''

''Riskier doing nothing.''

''Why don't you give Sherlock the Sheriff a call?''

''I don't trust him, Nate.''

''What do you need?''

''For you to make yourself scarce.''

''You got it, partner. You need me, though, I'm not far. Leave a message on the machine.''

''And do me a favor, Nate? Reach Hunt and Vicki.

And call the kid, Mike. Let them know what's going on and make sure they get scarce too for a while.''

''I'll take care of them, partner,'' he said and the line went dead.

I turned to Pat. ''We have to make you scarce, too.''

''I can take care of myself.''

''Not with this crowd.''

''I'm a tough woman.''

''Tough doesn't work against bombs and bullets, Pat. You're here with me tonight. Tomorrow we park you somewhere safe.''

The look on her face said she didn't like it. ''And you?''

''The guy at the mine all but invited me to take a look at his files. I think I'll take him up on that.''

Pat started to object but I covered her lips with my finger. ''Trust me, Pat. This time, you have to have some faith.''

IT WAS THE MIDDLE of the night when I knew they'd come for us. Pat was spooned into my back on the narrow bed breathing softly in sleep but I hadn't closed my eyes. The inky darkness outside was dead hushed quiet, not even a hint of a breeze stirring the pines. Then, from a far-off corner of the pasture I heard one of the horses blow a soft worried snort and I was instantly alert: that sound could only mean she'd sensed something in the darkness, something that shouldn't be out there. I sensed it too…something dark, something dangerous.

I gently slid my hand across Pat's limp mouth. She started up in panic and I choked off her cry of surprise. She came to quickly, realizing instantly what I was doing and nodding her head. I removed my hand and her dark eyes were wide in surprise and fear.

"Something's outside," I whispered in a voice so low it was almost inaudible. "Get your car keys and wait inside the door. If something happens to me, run. If you can make it to the car, go. If you can't, run for the woods. Understand?"

Pat nodded her head up and down, her eyes hardening. I padded softly to the sink and grabbed the filleting knife I'd used the night of the bear, wishing for the first time I still kept a gun.

Easing up to the front door, I stood frozen for a few seconds, listening for any sound from outside. There was nothing. Pat came noiselessly up beside and we exchanged a quick glance. I ran my hand lightly over her hair and then slid out the door.

It was cold and dead still in the darkness. I stood there with my back against the wall of the cabin for fully a minute, working to control my senses and accustom my eyes to the black night. No sounds around me, distant forms a confused jumble of meaningless shapes in the darkness. I slid silently to the end of the cabin and paused: from around the corner now I could just make out the almost imperceptible sounds of something breathing. Adrenaline swept through my body.

I swung around the corner a balled form of fury and movement, the knife straight out in front of me, lunging into the blackness. A human form grunted in surprise and fell backward and I was on him and my knife dug into flesh and bounced off bone. He staggered backward and I lunged at him again and he parried the thrust with a massive arm and his fist glanced off my temple and stars exploded behind my eyes. Another blow caught me squarely in the stomach and I staggered back a step or two and he was on me in a deadly sweaty embrace. I smelled stale beer on his breath and saw on his face something that looked like a mask of a tiger's head and then he had my knife hand in his two hands and I thought my wrist was breaking and the knife fell away and I brought my knee up into his groin and he hunched over stunned.

I brought my other hand up in a balled fist and hammered him in the face and he fell backward and I got a quick glance of Pat running toward her car but then the man was on me again and we fell heavily against the wall of the cabin and slid down into the dirt and the guy had his fingers in my face and was trying to poke my eyes out of their sockets. I managed to get both hands around his neck and was squeezing for everything I was worth and the man head-butted me and I fell back and he was up and running toward the woods.

I crawled to my feet and staggered after him and we were on the edge of the woods when the air around me seemed to disintegrate and something lifted me up and threw me bodily into the lower branches of the pines and the roar of an explosion behind me came crashing all around and knocked the wind from my chest.

Somehow I was on my face in the pine needles under the lower boughs of a tree and the night around me seemed to be alive with sounds: a car horn blaring from somewhere, birds screeching, horses neighing in panic, and a dull orange reflection of fire behind me. I turned painfully in the dirt to see small flames lapping at the corner of the cabin around a hole the size of a refrigerator that had been blown in the wall. From beyond, the flat terrifying drone of the car horn.

I crawled to my feet and ran across the lot. The windows of Pat's car were smashed in and her inert form lay across the steering wheel, her face against the horn. I wrenched the door open and pulled her out, laying her gently on her back on the ground and searching for a pulse. Her eyes opened and after a moment or two snapped into focus.

"Ben," she said, grabbing at me.

"It's all right," I said, folding her into my arms. "It's all right."

"What happened?"

"They blew us up. Some sort of bomb. I had the guy but he got away."

"Are you hurt?"

"Scratched is all. How 'bout you?"

She stood slowly with my help. "I think I'm okay. They blew us up?"

"They got the corner of the house." Pat's eyes followed my gaze toward the gaping hole and the slender fingers of flame licking at the logs.

"Who did it?" Her voice was a whisper.

"Same people who killed Summey," I said. "The same people who killed Woolsey."

TWENTY-FIVE

AT DAWN the next morning I put plywood sheets across the hole in my house and discovered a small pack with two more lumps of plastic explosives the killer hadn't had time to set. It would have killed us both.

At noon I checked Pat into a motel outside Missoula.

At sundown I drove up the mountain road toward the Rainbow Mine. I knew they'd be expecting me. My hope was they wouldn't be expecting me this soon.

About a mile short of the gate, I parked the pickup on an old logging road in a dense stand of heavy timber, grabbed a small pack and set off on foot up the face of the mountain toward the mine.

Heavy brush and the lack of good trails made it tough going. After an hour or so I lost the light and it slowed things even further. The gloom distorted shapes out of recognition and my nerves seemed to grow with every step I took upward. At one point I thought I could make out the shape of a man kneeling above me on the mountainside and froze in place for fully two minutes before I decided it was a tree trunk. Finally I came out on a small moss-covered ledge. Below and to my right maybe a quarter of a mile away

I could make out the mine's main gate. A single bare electric bulb glowed in the dark above the mesh fence and a dark pickup was parked nearby. Beyond, the main workings of the mine were lit here and there in the eerie blue of tungsten steel vapor lights. The trailers looked like long pale slugs hugging the ground. The ore pile loomed as a small dark mountain. A string of bright orange lights disappeared into the tunnel.

As I watched, an ore truck emerged and shunted its load of rock to the grate next to the mill and then turned back into the tunnel. Before long the crushing mill started up with a heavy throbbing roar that seemed to swallow the mountainside.

The lights went off in the office trailer about eight and a handful of people got in their cars and left. The guard at the front entrance emerged from his pickup to open the gate and wave them through. I watched him climb back in the truck, the dome light glowing dully for a few seconds. Sweaty palms, breathing tight. Eight-ten.

The crushing mill stopped its roar shortly after and two men emerged from a side door and disappeared into a nearby shack. The glowing dial of my wristwatch told me it took about two hours for the mill to process a load of ore.

I propped my back against a tree and settled down to watch the mine, time their schedules, and wait for my chance. Around me the forest was also settling in for the night. Somewhere to the south an owl punctuated the stillness with its long brown call. A little after eleven I heard something, probably a deer or a chipmunk, moving not far off in the brush but the sounds gradually went away.

At just about midnight another load of ore came out

and the crushing machine started up again. A few minutes after that the light in the guard's pickup shone for a few seconds and went out. The man emerged in the cone of light by the main gate where he stretched and rubbed the back of his head before walking away. I lost him in the darkness but a minute or so later caught the beam of his flashlight swinging along the steel fence, working clockwise around the perimeter. I checked the time and waited. It took the guy 28 minutes to complete the circuit around the mine's fences.

The pattern repeated itself again at two. Thirty minutes exactly for him to walk the perimeter fence. If the pattern held, I had an hour and a half to get into position. Taking a deep breath and steeling myself for what was to come, I eased off the ledge.

At 4:15 I'm on my belly in deep grass and deeper shadow about twenty feet from the steel fence. The crusher is roaring like a jet engine. I check my watch for the hundredth time. The guard should be coming past any second. It's a cold night, but I don't feel it. The crusher's so noisy I can scarcely hear myself think. But it's noise I need.

The flashlight beam is swinging back and forth in the dark, headed my way. I tuck down tighter in the grass and watch from squinted eyes. The guard's a dark shapeless form in the night, the flashlight a white needle in the darkness. The beam hits the fence and caroms off into the trees and grass—then back onto the fence, back into the trees. I draw down even deeper. The form passes by. The flashlight gets fainter. I do a final time check. Four-twenty. He won't be back for an hour and 40 minutes. The crusher should be working for another hour. Time to move, fast.

I do a quick dash to the fence and pull bolt cutters from my pack, ripping a body-sized hole in the wire. The snap of the jaws on wire isn't even faintly audible under the din of the crushing machine. I scramble through and take my bearings: I've come out just beyond the preg ponds to the rear of the giant ore pile. Staying well to the shadows, I hunch down and run past the ponds and around the side of the ore pile. At the far edge, I pause. No one around that I can see, trailer windows dark. No activity in the tunnel. I scuttle across the open area near the ore pile and flatten in darkness against the wall of the trailer that has the skull and crossbones on it. Still no one around. A fast dash now through a lighted area and I'm up against the door of the office trailer. I hit the lock with the liquid nitrogen. It cracks with a small pop but the door won't budge. I jam the jaws of the bolt cutters into the lock, wrenching them back and forth. A loud crack and it's open. I scramble inside and pull it closed behind me.

I'm crouched in the darkened trailer now, trying to catch my breath, get my nerves down to a manageable level. It's the same feeling I had on Summey's boat: breaking and entering scares me and I don't like it. I'm not going to do this again if I live through it this time. Not going to do it ever.

My eyes slowly adjust to the half light coming in through the windows. I'm in a long room. At one end two desks with computers, a computer printer, and a copying machine. Charts on the walls. At the other end a small table with folding chairs around it. Four filing cabinets nearly as tall as I. Each cabinet locked with a long steel rod fitted down through holes in the face and attached with a padlock at the base. Four-thirty.

I set the bolt cutters on the first padlock but they won't cut. The liquid nitrogen does the trick and the padlock cracks open with a snap clearly audible even above the roar of the crushing machine outside. I rummage in the pack for the flashlight and hold it in my teeth. The cabinet is stuffed with time sheets, personnel records. I pull a couple out and page through them quickly. Run-of-the-mill paperwork. More of the same in the next file. Frustratingly, the third drawer is still more. The fourth drawer down reveals police reports on employees—background investigations into the people hired by Rainbow. Orin Gacey's sheet with a passport photo attached. I pull it from the folder: Rainbow Mines' foreman, no criminal record, negative on drug tests. Jamming it back into the folder, I catch all but the briefest glimpse of another photo and my brain lurches and my heart goes skidding. Of course. Can I be that stupid? Of course. That's how they knew what I was doing. That's how they covered themselves moving equipment onto the two ranches. I pull the sheet halfway out of the file. The photo isn't very good. Black and white. As grim as a mug shot. And the way they've framed it you can't see her swelling chest and the tight black slacks and the long painted fingers without a wedding ring. You can't see her squeezing out a fake tear for a dead rancher. The way it's shot you can't pick up Roberta Feldy's low humming sexuality or the promise in her eyes, can't feel her hands at lunch stroking yours. Roberta Feldy. Westlands has been in it all along with Rainbow. Sure. Now it's as plain as the cuts on my knuckles. Westlands fronts for Rainbow. They know all the big ranches, all the old gold mines. They go in and do deals with the owners and Rainbow sneaks in the back door. And they hide the records, the paperwork, the gun whose smoke would convict them, in an innocuous file cabinet in a mine no one would ever connect up with the ranches and the slick agro business. I slide the sheet back into the folder, feeling a cold hollow anger.

Four forty-five and the next cabinet. Production reports which I don't take time to read. Purchase orders and receipts. A file marked simply "Sula." I pull it out and lay it on the floor. In front of me in the narrow beam of the flashlight a stack of papers: Gordon Technology, the tight legalese, Joe Summey's scrawled signature at the bottom. It's a copy of the contract I found on Summey's boat. Old news. I dig further. Another contract: Woolsey's name printed on the front page. And then another name...I take a quick breath in astonishment and read it again. So that's it, that's how they got to Woolsey, of course—it'd be easy that way. Their secret little mole deep in the operation, their secret agent doing their bidding, biding their time. Of course...and I jump almost out of my skin as the light above me switches on in a blinding glare and I whirl and a huge ugly man with a tattooed face and a seeping bandage on his arm has a pistol pointed at my eyes.

"Told you once to stay away," the man snarls above the sound of the crusher. "Now guess it don't matter, huh?" He cocks the trigger with an exaggerated movement of his thumb and I flinch backward against the metal files, my eyes stuttering between the barrel of the pistol and the bizarre tattoo that spreads like some disease from his collar and across his jaws

nearly to his eyes. A black and yellow animal's face—
maybe a tiger—and in its strangeness even more terrifying than the gun pointed at me. I realize I've seen
it before, three times, but didn't know what it was
then. Once I was being kicked to death in an alley and
twice I was fighting for my life in the dirt outside my
cabin.

I raise my hands slowly, careful not to make a sudden move and invite a bullet into my face. "Let's not
do something stupid," I say but the words are lost
beneath the din of the crushing mill and, besides, I'd
already been the one to do that something stupid.

The man takes a half step forward and jabs the gun
toward me. "Turn around and lean against the files."

I do as I'm told and now with my back to the man
feel even more vulnerable than before. The steel muzzle is pressing into the soft hollow spot in the back of
my skull. A thought flashes through my head that this
is how the Chinese execute people. The guy pats me
down from head to foot looking for a gun. His pistol
keeps me hanging there against the files like an insect
pinned to a board.

And there we stay: a gun pressed into the back of
my head, a man with a tiger's face behind me, a roar
like hell itself all around. A minute, maybe more. It
could have been an hour for all I know as my mind
rushes through a kaleidoscopic reel of dumb fear and
blind anger. Of all the scrapes I'd been in, all the tight
spots where life itself was a game of considered
chance and dumb luck, it seemed now so stupid that
it might end like this. Huge anger at the man behind
me...but even more anger at myself for taking this
obvious risk, for thinking I was stronger, quicker,
smarter—that there wasn't a fix I couldn't get myself

out of. Maybe, finally, I've taken one risk too many. But did I have a choice? Was there another way? I couldn't see it...but my vision is narrowed considerably by the presence of soft lead three inches from my skin waiting to liquefy the tissue of my brain and snuff out my existence. I think of Pat.

"So you accepted our invitation, huh?" It's a new voice behind me. Familiar. The voice of our mine guide from a couple of days before, Gacey. "Turn around."

The muzzle pressure eases off and I turn slowly. Gacey is standing there in khakis and red hard hat, one hand knotted in a tight fist, the other closed around a large automatic pistol. A mean expression on his face. "You're none too smart," he shouts over the noise. I'm nodding in agreement. "Couldn't stay away, huh?" His mouth forms a narrow nasty grin. "I figured you for a sucker. Didn't know how right I was. But see, having you here is where we want you. No trace that way."

He turns slightly to the tattooed man next to him: "Bring him out, and be careful. Does anything stupid, kill him." With that Gacey turns and the other guy comes around behind me and gives me a shove toward the door with the barrel of the gun jabbed between my shoulder blades.

The crushing mill is still sending out its infernal roar as Gacey leads us to one of the ore carriers and gestures Tattoo into the driver's seat. Gacey gestures me up into the cab and climbs in next to me, keeping the pistol trained roughly in the direction of my nose, an unreadable expression on his face. Tattoo starts up the machine and we drive across the lot and edge into the tunnel. Just inside the entrance the roar of the crusher eases and Gacey tells Tattoo to pull up and stop.

"You're stupid," says Gacey. "Should've kept out of it."

I try to say something but Gacey thrusts the pistol almost into my eye and I duck back.

"Shut up," he snarls. "You played with us on this one. Now we play with you."

"You kill Summey?" I manage to say.

He just laughs.

"How'd you make me?"

The snarl again. "Look in your rearview mirror once in a while? Be surprised who's back there."

Gacey looks past me at the driver. "I've got business." A look of understanding passes between the two. "Take this fella into the north drift and blow 'em up. Then seal it." Tattoo nods like it's a routine request and Gacey swings down out of the cab. "Have a nice short life," he says and disappears out of the tunnel.

Tattoo levels his pistol at my face and pulls back the hammer with his thumb. The bandage on his arm is oozing blood. "Real simple," he says. "You move, you die." With that he shifts the big ore carrier into gear and we head down the tunnel.

The light of the electric bulbs dies away behind us and along with it the noise of the crushing mill. Now just the steady throb of the truck's engine as we move along at a slow jog. In the dull reflected glow from the machine's headlights the man has the gun face-level to me and his finger is on the trigger.

"It was you in the alley, right?"

The man nods his head and grunts.

"And then again at my cabin?"

Another nod.

"You kill Woolsey?"

No response.

"You kill Summey?"

"Shut up," he says, his eyes about halfway between me and the tunnel road ahead of us.

It's a stupid question but I ask it anyway: "What now?"

He doesn't answer.

We reach the first junction in the tunnel that I remember from the time before. The light swells for a minute as we pass under an electric bulb and then we're swallowed again in the gloom. The gun is steady on my face and my mind's whirling and it's like a dark jagged nightmare and I'm feeling the anger swell in my chest. This guy and his pals, they'd found gold in the hills, done deals with those willing to deal, and killed an old man who stood in their way. Then when things got nasty they killed again. A company that was probably a member of the Chamber of Commerce, with lawyers in fancy suits in Manhattan doing big power deals, stockholders at annual meetings in posh hotels, limos, private planes, the perks of the elite. And they'd killed an old man living alone in the Montana mountains. For what? For the few pennies it would add to an annual report? They'd snuffed out a long decent life for a few more bucks on the bottom line, for a few more five-star restaurants and Cuban cigars. An old man froze to death at the bottom of a gully so they could go around and find more mines and kill a few more old men. And it wasn't really about money, it was about power. The powerful had killed the powerless. To them probably a faceless cipher on a field report turned in by some loyal maggot like Gacey who knew more money would bring more power.

The anger holds there steady, like a steel beam next to my heart. The gun still level in my face, I begin to breathe shallowly, relaxing the muscles of my arms and legs, centering my mind and stripping away all other thoughts.

A few more minutes down the tunnel and we're coming to another fork. The man next to me takes his hand off the wheel and shifts down one gear. The pistol is now waist-high pointed at my belly. I'm barely breathing. He moves his hand back to the wheel and his eyes jog off and in that instant I uncoil all at once and dive to my left and kick upward with both feet. My boot hits the man's wrist and the gun fires with a lightning crack and in less than a heartbeat I'm out of the truck and running into the swallowing darkness. An engine screams into high and then a couple of shots and I feel the slugs whistle by and slam into the hard rock of the tunnel wall. I'm running as fast as I can move my legs, my heart pumping, adrenaline shooting through my system like a million small rockets. More shots from behind and the bullets tear off the walls with a screaming lethal whine and I duck and keep running and soon I'm swallowed in complete blackness. I can still hear the engine behind me. The darkness is now absolute—an inky blackness where I can't see my fist in front of my face, a consuming, claustrophobic blackness that is at once my friend and my enemy.

I slow to a trot and feel my way along the tunnel wall like a blind man in a maze. I keep up the pace for what seems like a lifetime but it's probably no

more than a couple of minutes. Behind me, the sound
of the ore carrier seems to be getting closer.

Ahead, suddenly, a snatch of dim light and I break
into a flat-out run. The junction we'd passed on the
way in. I shoot through it and then skid to a stop. I
still have a long way to go to get to the entrance and
freedom, maybe as much as half a mile, all up hill—
and he's gaining behind me. I turn down the other
tunnel, back toward the heart of the mine. Maybe it
will give me room to maneuver if he thinks I'm
headed toward the front. I run maybe two hundred
yards into the inky darkness and throw myself up
against the wall, gasping for breath and trying to hear
where he's headed. The big engine grows in my ears
and then abruptly shifts down to idle. He's at the junction. If he turns back toward the center of the mine,
back in my direction, I've nowhere to run. I stand
there frozen in sweat and adrenaline. A few seconds
and then the engine fires back up. He's headed my
way. Instant panic. I stumble along the tunnel wall
expecting to feel a bullet rip into my back, but
then...then the engine seems to be getting fainter. I
stop. The engine noise is receding, going away. He's
turned down the tunnel toward the entrance. I'm alone.
A few minutes and the sound dies entirely and all I
can hear is my own heart pumping in my chest. I'm
grateful it's still pumping.

The blind rush of action gives way slowly to reason.
I am in a mine with only one way out. The man will
look for me outside and not find me. He'll know I'm
still in the mine and he'll come back. And I will die.
As simple as that: I have to get out. In the utter darkness, I find the tunnel wall with my hands and then

begin jogging in the direction I hope will lead me toward the main entrance.

It's maybe ten minutes before a dim light ahead tells me I've gone the right way. I slow and edge even closer to the wall. The entrance area looks clear—I can see the ore carrier idling in the lot just beyond, empty. No sign of Gacey or the man with the tattooed face. I flatten against the cold stone wall and stick my head around the edge: The crushing mill is still in full roar. No humans anywhere. I pause to catch my breath. Maybe if I can hug the dark face of the mountain and make my way to the fence, I can jump over and disappear into the heavy forest beyond.

I take a few deep breaths, willing myself to be like a comet, and then sprint out of the entrance. A muzzle flash erupts instantly in front of me and I hear the faint crack of a shot. I lurch around and make for the buildings, another shot popping just behind. I run for all I'm worth and duck around the side of a trailer, still apparently in one piece. No time to stop. I dash across an open space and disappear around behind the blast shack with its skull and crossbones. I hear a shout behind me above the roar of the mill and angle off in a fast low crouch toward the massive ore pile, hoping to dissolve into its shadow.

I come around the side of the mill building in full run. In front of me a long open space stretches out between the crushing mill and the ponds of cyanide. I can't do it: too much of a target for too long in the open. I dash back down along the mill and duck into a dark spot in steel wall just feet from the edge of the black and acrid pond. The tattooed man comes around the corner, his gun out in front of him in two hands swinging back and forth like the guard's flashlight. He

doesn't see me. I wait. He comes up in front of me in
the open, his back toward me and I dive. We roll into
the dirt and the gun skitters away. I try grabbing him
around the neck and he shakes free and gets me in the
side of the head with a club-like smash of his fist and
stars briefly swim in my eyes.

I roll to the side and kick into his legs and we both
crab backward and struggle to our feet, circling each
other now like a couple of sumo wrestlers. He charges
first, head down, fists out front swinging for my face.
I dodge to the side and get in a clumsy shot to his
nose. He staggers backward, blood pouring down his
face. Another charge and I dodge to the side but not
fast enough as his leg sweeps under mine and I feel
myself jerked off my feet. I land hard on the flat of
my back and am momentarily without breath and he
pounces on me, one arm up under my neck, his free
hand gouging into my face and my eyes. I try squirm-
ing away but his weight is too great. I blade my hands
and chop them down into the back of his neck with
all my strength. The pressure of his hands eases for
just an instant but it's enough: I'm out from under him
and rolling to my feet.

We stand there facing each other, both of us gasping
for breath, and he lunges. This time I stand my ground
and meet him with a feinted left and then a hard right
into the center of his face just above the nose. I feel
an instant of searing pain in my hand and know I've
broken some fingers. He staggers back and slumps to
his knees. I kick him in the gut as hard as I can and
he topples backward and rolls down the bank toward
the chemical pond, his inert form sliding down the
slick plastic and sinking backward into the chemical
soup.

I kneel and catch my breath, arguing with myself about whether I ought to keep him alive. At length I bend over and slowly pull his unconscious bulk out of the deadly cyanide and lay him out on the plastic fringe. I sit there for a minute gasping for breath and trying to collect my wits and then slowly rise to my feet.

And, somehow, the man comes at me again, hitting me behind the knees with a low body block. I tumble into the dirt and his boot smashes into my side with a blinding burst of pain. I roll over and try to find my feet but my legs don't seem to be working. And he's coming toward me, a snarl of hatred etched into his bizarre painted mouth and he kicks at my head with a round-house karate move and I manage to catch his leg with both hands and suddenly he's airborne and comes crashing down on the edge of the black pond. I stagger up as he crawls to his knees and without even thinking about it I lash out with a tremendous kick that takes him directly in the tiger's whiskers and sends him reeling backward into the cyanide. He struggles in the liquid, his arms flailing, his eyes wide and he's screaming but I can barely hear it over the roar of the crushing mill. He sinks once and then bobs up again spewing cyanide from his mouth and windmilling his arms. I sit there breathing hard, not moving. He screams again and then sinks below the black waves in a fury of lashing arms and kicking feet. This time he doesn't come back up.

The pond settles, the ripples die away, and I gasp for breath and cradle my broken fingers. The crushing mill stops and the night is swallowed in silence and I feel myself sliding toward some huge darkness and struggle to fight it off. I know what has to be done. I hope I'm not too late.

TWENTY-SIX

THE SUN IS edging up over the eastern mountains as I fishtail the pickup into the street and coast to a stop. A half block away, the house sits in deep shadow, the curtains down over the windows, no signs of life.

I park the truck and make my way slowly, cautiously, down the street, my senses sharp, my eyes scanning up and down the block. My fingers ache but I push the thought aside and creep up silently to the front door. It's locked. I stand there listening for any sounds from within, but there's nothing. I move around the side of the house and down a brick patio to a rear door. Locked as well. A black and white cat watches me from the edge of the lawn. The air feels tight, edgy.

Back at the front door I listen again for maybe a minute. No sounds from within. I hit the buzzer. Nothing. I hit it again and leave my finger on it this time for maybe 20 seconds. It sounds like a drill inside the house. I hear movement. The curtain edges back and Ed Woolsey's worried unshaven face appears at the door.

"You?" he says, his voice muffled by the thickness of the door.

"There's trouble. Are you okay?"

"Why wouldn't I be?" He's trying to rub sleep from his eyes.

"Let me in."

"What is it?"

"Just let me in."

"Get away from me."

"People are dying. Open the door."

Woolsey hesitates for a moment then I hear movement in the lock and the door swings open. I push in quickly, shouldering past him, glancing around the small office. "Are you okay?"

Woolsey gives me a bleary-eyed stare and runs his hand through his thin white hair. "Why shouldn't I be?"

"Your wife here?"

"What?"

"Where's your wife."

Woolsey points toward a door, an empty, frightened look growing on his face. "Bedroom," he says.

I push into a small living room and through an open door beyond can see a rumpled bed. Mrs. Woolsey is sitting halfway up, the sheets around her chin, her face white and terrified. "Out fast," I order but she doesn't move. "Game's up," I hiss, "and they're coming after you. Now get up and move it!" She bolts from the bed in her pajamas and starts to run past me. I grab at her and suddenly we both jump at the sounds of shattering glass and shouts from the front of the house. I whirl as Ed Woolsey's form comes stumbling backward into the living room, Orin Gacey behind him, a snarl on his lips and the big pistol in his fist straight out in front of him. Ed falls against a chair and slumps to the floor, his arms up across his face. Mrs. Woolsey is backing up toward the wall, her face a mask of terror, her eyes on the barrel of the gun.

"So all of you in one room, huh?" snarls Gacey. "Makes it easy, doesn't it?"

"What the..." It's Woolsey, his voice a whimper.

"Careful who you marry," says Gacey. "Some of them turn out to be black widows." He barks out a thin, sharp laugh and swings the gun level with the woman's face. She screams and flattens against the wall.

Woolsey looks toward me, uncomprehending terror in his eyes.

"Married the wrong woman," I say. "She sold you out."

Woolsey's gaze darts back to his wife.

"Did a deal with the miners," I say, "and set your father up to die."

"Louise?" Woolsey's voice sounds like it's strangling.

"I saw the documents," I say. "As soon as you got the land, you'd be a dead man too. She'd take it all."

"Louise?" says Woolsey again, the word a mix of plea and question.

"You really had no idea?" sneers Gacey. "Sleeping all these years with the little lady and still you didn't know? Dumb sucker, aren't you? Minute we even suspected there was gold up there, she was on us like a blood sucker. S'pect she knew there wasn't much future in insurance." Gacey cocks the trigger on the gun.

"Doesn't do any good," I say. "Too many people know."

Gacey squeezes the trigger and the shot explodes like a cannon in the small room. The woman's body jerks back into the wall like a rag doll. Woolsey screams and I dive for the gun and hit Gacey's arm and we fall backward over a table and hit the floor in a tangle of arms and curses and grunts. Gacey knees me in the stomach and I stagger back. He brings the pistol up and I hit his arm as he squeezes the trigger and the shot takes out a window behind my shoulder and I lunge for the pistol and get it in both hands and we struggle in a slow heaving lethal dance across the floor, our four hands on the gun. He looks at me and sneers and I feel his finger tightening on the trigger and I manage to jerk his wrist as he squeezes off a shot and it thumps hollowly into the plaster of the wall but my broken fingers won't hold the grip and he wrenches his hands free and we twist and stumble to the side and I'm falling back against a sofa and there's another shot and I cringe at the concussion and Woolsey is screaming from somewhere in the confusion and the sheriff has come out of nowhere and is moving into the room, his big pistol out in both hands aimed directly at Gacey's face.

"Put the gun down!" the sheriff screams.

Gacey is smiling, his eyes half closed, almost like he's dreaming.

"Drop it now!" yells the sheriff again.

Gacey raises his arms slowly at his sides and the gun slips from his fingers and drops with a loud thump to the floor.

The sheriff swings his gun like a flashlight across me and then across Woolsey and the woman's bloody form and then brings the pistol back eye-level on Gacey. "Are you hurt?" he says to me without taking his eyes off Gacey.

"I'm okay."

"Call 911."

I crawl to my feet.

The sheriff barks out commands to Gacey: "Turn around and lean against the wall."

"How'd you know?" I ask.

"Your friend the doctor," says the sheriff.

I find the phone and start to dial and behind me there's a crash and the sheriff is falling backward and his gun is flying across the room and Gacey is scrambling on all fours toward it and the sheriff smashes into me and we're both on the floor and Gacey finds the gun and squeezes off a wild shot and I launch myself across the room and hit the floor in a rolling ball, scooping up the other gun with my good hand and Gacey is lining up his pistol on the sheriff and in the edge of a heartbeat I bring my hand up with the big gun in it and center Gacey's ear just above the bead and squeeze off a single shot. The side of Gacey's head disappears in a red mist and he drops to the floor like a stone, twitches once, and then goes still.

TWENTY-SEVEN

THE THIN YELLOW LINE flew out over the stream, hanging there for an instant before dropping softly onto the dappled water. I steadied Pat's arm as she brought the tip of the fly rod up and the current bit into the line. The fly eddied over a small rapids and drew up on a pool of still water. A flash and a quick roil of water. The tip of the pole bent forward and Pat jerked it back.

"Too slow," I said.

The line went slack and Pat turned to me grinning. "Another rainbow lives to fight another day."

"You had 'em."

"A trout's best friend," said Pat, her dark eyes glowing. "They know they're safe when I'm around." She laughed softly and cast the line out again. "Pour the wine, cowboy."

I waded out of the stream and sat down on the grassy bank, watching Pat's body move back and forth in the rhythm of casting. Her form had a supple, natural ease that seemed to fit perfectly into the stillness of the moment and the golden grace of the afternoon sun as it slid toward the mountains.

After a while she reeled in the line and waded out of the stream, water sloshing in her wet sneakers as she sat down beside me on the grass.

"Have you ever actually caught a fish on a fly rod?" Her eyes were mischievous.

"Big ones."

"I'll bet."

"The size of turkeys."

"I swear to God you and Bowen have made lying about fish into an art form." She smiled and lay back on the grass, cradling the wine glass on her stomach. My mind flashed back to a similar scene more than a month before when I'd given her the shot of whiskey on my narrow bed, the night Rainbow's man with the tattooed face tried to kill us.

"Hey Tripp, you're clouding over."

"Sorry."

"Still tender, isn't it?"

I nodded.

"For both of us," she said. "I guess it's probably like a head injury—it takes a while to go away. Like rhumba lessons." Pat was quiet for a time, her eyes staring up through the pines above us. "You haven't told me about the hearing."

"They're asking for the death penalty," I said and described the scene the day before in the courtroom in Missoula: Louise Woolsey in a wheelchair at the defense table as her young lawyer argued she hadn't known the old man would die that cold winter day, that it had been meant only to scare him. Louise Woolsey, a fundamentally good woman caught up innocently in a web of intrigue and evil in which she played no part.

Louise Woolsey watching from quick, frightened eyes as the prosecutor took his turn and laid out the government's case: the prosecution would prove, he said, that Louise Woolsey was anything but a good, innocent woman, that she had been in on it all from the beginning six or even seven years before; her first husband had been the realtor who handled the very first call when Rainbow Mines—or Gordon Technology, or Westlands, take your pick, they're all the same thing—came sniffing around on a suspicion there might be gold in the mountains; that even then, six years before, Louise Woolsey had begun laying her bloody plans to trade lives for a chunk of those mountains.

The prosecutor dropped a thick stack of papers on the table in front of him and told the court that this behaviour wasn't new for Louise Woolsey. In this pile, he said, are convictions for grand theft larceny—she did two years in an Illinois prison for that—and another for manslaughter, a year on that. All under a different name, in a different place far away. Closer to home, though, the police should have been more interested when her first husband died in what appeared to be a hunting accident. It was no accident.

Whirling in the courtroom and pointing his finger directly at Louise Woolsey, the prosecutor said that her husband's murder was the first step in this bloody trail. He'd led her to the gold but his honesty stood in the way of her collecting it. So he had to be disposed of. A convenient hunting accident. And even before she married Ed Woolsey this woman had come up with a lethal plan to inherit his ranch and his part of the mountain. That plan meant that two more men— her new husband and her new father-in-law—would have to die, but in Louise Woolsey's twisted mind, that was not a large price to pay to make the mountain of gold hers.

Louise Woolsey, sitting there in the sterile courtroom as the prosecutor told how she'd introduced Carson Woolsey to Westlands and convinced him to let them run the ranch—and then had lied and covered as his suspicions grew. Louise Woolsey, who talked him out of selling the ranch.

Ed Woolsey at the back of the courtroom with a hard and hating look. The prosecutor explaining how the woman had lured Carson Woolsey to his death with a phone call. They'd traced the records. One call made that day to Carson Woolsey from a cellphone belonging to Louise Woolsey. The prosecutor didn't know, couldn't prove, what had been said in that call, it would forever remain a mystery—unless Louise Woolsey chose to tell the court. Whatever she said to him that cold winter day, it had been enough to lure an old man out into a blizzard and to his death. A miner with a tattooed face had been the actual instrument of murder. But it was Louise Woolsey who had wielded that instrument as surely as if she had wielded the club that had done the killing. All part of the deal. One old man dead, one more man to go and the ranch would be hers. But then it started to unravel. A young man suspecting his grandfather would not die so foolishly had started asking questions, and Louise Woolsey and the rest of them had scurried to hide their golden trail of murder. A lump of Rainbow plastic explosives had dispatched Joe Summey and his unsuspecting companion to a watery grave. Another lump had almost killed an investigator asking difficult questions. The prosecutor vowed they all would hang.

"You okay?" Pat's voice, bringing me back around.

"Twisted woman."

"She is that," said Pat. "What about the other one, the one from Westlands?"

"Accessory to murder," I said and Roberta Feldy's face swam through my mind: the lunch we'd had, the tight slacks and fire-engine-red blouse over the astonishing chest. The bottle of wine left on my table. The half-promises. The hints. The flirting. And all the time her one job had been to keep an eye on me—and let the others know when it was time for me to die. "Prison, probably." I wondered if her looks would survive 10 or 20 years in the state pen. I realized I didn't care.

"The rest?" said Pat. "Rainbow, Gordon Technology, that whole crowd?"

"Still out there. Hiding behind a wall of lawyers. The prosecutor says they'll fall too. But I wonder."

"They almost got away with it."

"Almost," I said.

"I feel sorry for Summey."

Summey. The old rancher with the patrician look and the Shakespearean manner. The canvas with the brown lines of the mountains and the small patch of blue. His hatred for the Montana winters—and the cold colors of frozen death.

"He was never really in it, was he?"

I shook my head. "Looks like he made a deal with them and then shut up. The sheriff says there's nothing tying him to Woolsey's death."

"The sheriff," said Pat.

"Interesting man," I said. "He was at the hearing. As creased as ever—and as humorless."

"He ever thank you for saving his life?"

"He did. Awkward, but he managed it."

"I think they're coming."

I followed Pat's gaze downstream. Bowen and Mike were wading along the shore on the far side of the creek, their poles over their shoulders. As we watched, Bowen brought his fly rod up and cast out into the center of the flow. Mike duplicated the movement precisely with his own line. The two of them stood as still as statues as the lines eddied and whirled with the current.

"I was in court yesterday, too," said Pat, shyly, her eyes firmly on the water.

"And...?"

"And I'm Pat Gonzales again."

"Pat Gonzales. I like that."

"Long overdue," she said softly.

I touched her shoulder and she turned her gaze back to me. "Long overdue," I said and brushed my lips across hers.

A cat whistle from across the stream. I looked up. Bowen and the boy were watching us. Bowen started clapping his hands.

"Some people's friends," said Pat, smiling.

"Not my friends," I said and kissed her again, this time a little harder.

The clapping stopped and Bowen and the boy went back to fishing.

"And so what about Ben Tripp?" said Pat.

"What about him?"

"I don't know. I mean, what now?"

"Finish the bedroom, I guess. Patch up the cabin. Get on with things."

"Things?"

"The things I do."

"And those are?"

"Well, you see, I've met this pretty girl. Lives

down the road a piece, but that shouldn't be a problem. She's a doctor, you know, so she doesn't have all that much time in her life. But I'm kind of figuring I'm going to wedge my way in there, see what happens.''

''Sounds like a good plan.''

''I think so.''

''I think I know this doctor you're talking about,'' said Pat, her eyes shining. ''Works too hard. Doesn't even have time to go to dinner. I hear, though, that she'd like to change some of those ways.'' Pat smiling. ''Word is she met a cowboy, drives an old pickup.''

''Quite a guy, I hear.''

''Quite a guy,'' said Pat.

The two of us kissed again and dropped into silence.

On the canyon wall across from us, a patch of pines had picked up the afternoon sun and was glowing almost yellow-green against the dark forest around it. Not too far away, I knew, there was another place—a small patch of earth along an empty stretch of road—where the new grass was budding out in the same colors of regeneration and triumph as nature began the ancient process of covering over her new wounds. I hugged Pat to my chest and let my eyes wash across the treeline, offering a silent shallow nod to an old man who had owned a ranch up in those mountains.